WEST INDIAN
FOLK-TALES

West Indian Folk-tales

Retold by
PHILIP SHERLOCK

Illustrated by
JOAN KIDDELL-MONROE

OXFORD UNIVERSITY PRESS
OXFORD TORONTO MELBOURNE

Oxford University Press, Walton Street, Oxford OX2 6DP

Oxford New York Toronto
Delhi Bombay Calcutta Madras Karachi
Petaling Jaya Singapore Hong Kong Tokyo
Nairobi Dar es Salaam Cape Town
Melbourne Auckland

and associated companies in
Berlin Ibadan

Oxford is a trade mark of Oxford University Press

First published 1966
Reprinted 1973, 1975, 1978, 1981
First published in paperback 1983
Reprinted 1985, 1987, 1988, 1989, 1990

ISBN 0-19-274127-6

Printed and bound in Great Britain by
Biddles Ltd, Guildford and King's Lynn

Author's Note

THE TIGER

The true tiger is not found in West Africa. It is likely, as the artist has indicated, that the tiger of the Anansi stories is a leopard. In her introduction to Walter Jekyll's *Jamaican Song and Story*, Alice Werner wrote in 1907: 'All over South Africa, leopards are called "tigers" by Dutch, English, and Germans, just as hyenas are called "wolves", and bustards "peacocks" . . . "Tiger" is used in the same sense in German Kamerun, and probably elsewhere in West Africa.'

Acknowledgements

Tiger Story, *Anansi Story*, and *Work-Let-Me-See* are based on the stories 'From Tiger to Anansi' and 'Brother Breeze and the Pear Tree', from the book *Anansi, the Spider Man*, copyright © 1954 by the author, Philip M. Sherlock. Used by permission of the publishers, Thomas Y. Crowell Company, New York, and Macmillan and Co. Ltd., London.

I gratefully acknowledge my indebtedness for the Carib stories to the Rev. Henry Brett, whose *Indian Tribes of Guiana* was published in London in 1868 by Bell and Daldy, and to Mrs. St. Aubyn who kindly let me read her version of some of the stories.

For some of the Anansi stories I drew on Walter Jekyll's excellent collection *Jamaican Song and Story*, published for the English Folklore Society, London, 1907.

I am grateful also to the Institute of Jamaica, and especially to its West Indies Reference Library.

CONTENTS

From Sun-Spirit to Spider-Man

A TIME came when the Arawak people, and their cousins the Caribs, wandered far from the shadow of Mount Roraima. Some settled in the broad land we now call Guyana. Others moved north to the banks of the Orinoco River and the shores of the Gulf of Paria.

From the mainland the Arawaks who lived by the Gulf of Paria and the mouth of the Orinoco, could see, pencilled against the sky, the shapes of mountains. The old men were content to stay where they were, but the young men longed to cross the Gulf to the distant mountains. From the giant trees of the forest they made dug-out canoes, each so large that it required fifty or sixty men to drive it through the heaving waters with their oars. In these dug-out canoes they crossed from the mainland to the islands, to Trinidad, and Tobago, which still bears the Arawak name for tobacco, and Barbados and Grenada.

As the generations passed, the Arawaks, and the Caribs at a later time, moved from island to island in their dug-out canoes, settling even in those islands that lay farthest north, Jamaica and Cuba, and Haiti the land of mountains, and in the islands that we now call the Bahamas.

In these islands of the Caribbean the Arawaks and Caribs made their homes. They lived in villages near the sea, searched the shores for chip-chip and mussels, fished with hooks of bone or shell, hunted in the woods for the iguana and coney, and cultivated maize, cassava, and sweet-potatoes. Not knowing the use of iron they made tools from stone, bone, and shells. For weapons they had spears and arrows tipped with bone, shell, or sharp flint. From generation to generation they passed on stories that their fathers had told, tales of the Ancient One who lived in the heights, and of the sun-spirit Arawidi who sometimes fished in the rivers of Guyana, and of the giant Coomacka-Tree that grew till its branches touched the sky.

For many centuries these Arawaks and Caribs of the islands lived as their fathers had done, in a world in which there was little change. The Arawaks, who were quiet, peaceful people, feared the fierce, warlike Caribs. They feared also the god Huracan, who brought storms in the summer, whipping the seas and tearing the branches from the forest trees in his anger. But they feared little else. They knew the changes of the year, the dry summer months and the wet rainy months, the seasons when the sapodillas and sweet sops ripened in

2

the woods, and the best times for planting maize and cassava. In their world it was always spring or summer. The trees were always green, the air gentle and warm. Year followed year, century followed century with little change. The old men and the old women fell asleep, and the young men and young women lived in the way their fathers had lived.

Then a strange thing happened. On the morning of Friday, October 12, in the year 1492, some Arawaks living in the little island of Guanahani in the Bahamas saw three canoes lying off-shore, larger than any canoes they had ever seen, each moved not by oars but by white wings. Men came ashore from the strange ships, but men such as they had never seen, with white-and-pink faces, bearded, their bodies covered with thick garments of cloth and with hard, bright metal. Once ashore the strangers fell on their knees, lifted their hands to the sky, kissed the ground, shouted for joy, and gathered round their leader, Christopher Columbus.

This was the first meeting between the old world of America and the old world of Europe. The two groups faced each other on the sandy beach: naked brown-skinned men with weapons of stone and shells, and white men from Europe, clad in armour, with weapons of iron. The Arawaks, whose fathers had crossed the gulf that lay between the mainland and the islands in their dug-out canoes, faced Spanish seamen who had crossed in their sailing-ships the wide gulf of the Atlantic that lay between Europe and the islands of the Caribbean.

The man of the iron age made the man of the stone age his servant, forcing him to labour like a slave, driving him to mine the earth for gold and silver,

3

making him give up the way of life to which he had been born. Each had crossed the wide gulf of the seas, but there was another gulf that lay between them, a gulf that only pity and understanding could bridge. But the greed of the iron-age man drove out pity, and the gulf was never bridged. The Arawaks perished, killed by new diseases and by cruelty. The Caribs perished also, but more slowly, being hardier than the Arawaks. A few hundred of them live in the island of Dominica to this day. Kinsmen of the Arawaks and Caribs live still in the savannahs of Guyana and in the basin of the Orinoco, but no Arawaks survive in the islands.

What people took the place of the first island folk, the Caribs and Arawaks? What legends do they tell in the islands where once the Arawaks listened to the stories of the Coomacka-Tree and of the sun-spirit Arawidi?

From across the Atlantic the Europeans brought by force men and women from the lands of West Africa to the islands of the Caribbean and to the mainland. For more than three hundred years ships crossed and re-crossed the Atlantic, laden with men and women brought to tame the forests and lay out plantations of sugar-cane and to make the sugar that Europe wanted.

In this way it came about that Africa moved across the Atlantic to the islands of the Caribbean. In this way it came about that most of the people of the islands are of African blood, with memories of ancient people and far-away lands, of Ashanti-land, and Dahomey, Congo-land and Iboland, of the Yorubas, the Fanti, and the Mandingo people.

Because of this forced movement of people from West

Africa to the islands, country folk in Haiti sing songs about Africa, like the song about an old man who once made up his mind to go back on a visit to the land from whence he came. After setting off he finds that he has forgotten his walking-stick, and so he sings:

> '*I am going to Africa*
> *When I get down the road I find you made me*
> *   forget my walking-stick . . .*'

And in Cuba a poet asks:

> '*Do I not have*
> *A night-stained forefather*
> *Bearing a great black brand . . .*'

And at evening in Jamaica and Barbados, Antigua and Trinidad, Grenada and Guyana, some old man tells stories about Anansi the spider, Tiger and Dog, Peafowl and Parrot, Monkey and Puss.

In Twi, one of the chief languages of West Africa, the word for spider is 'Ananse'; and the spider is the chief character in the folk-tales of the Ashanti people. Often he takes human shape, walks with a limp, and speaks with a lisp. A little bald-headed man with a falsetto voice, he lives by his wits, getting the better of Dog and Cat and most of the other animals by his cunning; though occasionally one of the animals gets the better of him. Yet, despite his greed and selfishness, there is something satisfying in the way in which Anansi outwits those much stronger and more powerful than himself, like Tiger and huge Assonoo, the elephant.

Most of the Anansi stories told in the islands are of

5

local origin. They are set in the West Indian landscape, and tell of animals that, with one or two exceptions, belong to the islands: parrot, blackbird, peafowl, puss, tumble-bug, snake, lizard, turtle, Old Conch the snail, cat, dog, and rat. Lively, dramatic, witty, the stories explain why many things in the world are as they are: why wasps sting, why dogs' bellies are hollow, why the spider lives in a web, and why monkey is a follow-fashion; and always at the centre of this world of dusk and enchantment is Anansi.

The Coomacka-Tree

THE Caribs were the first people. There were no other people before them. Their first home was the moon. They knew light and dark, day and night, and they obeyed the Ancient One, Kabo Tano.

In the bright procession of worlds that moved around them the Caribs saw one that never gleamed with light, but remained veiled by a thick, grey haze that grew duller and greyer with each passing season. If at times the veil lifted for a brief period there stood revealed bleak mountain peaks rising out of inky darkness.

The oldest Carib pointed to the dark, spinning earth and said to his youngest grandchild, 'It's a dull earth. It needs cleaning.'

A young Carib girl, combing her long black hair, pointed to the earth and said, 'It seems to get duller and duller. What that earth needs is a good polishing.'

The strongest of the young men among the Caribs of the Moon asked his companions, 'How can we put up year after year with this dull earth? Other generations have done nothing about it. Let us show what we can do. Our strength can transform the dull earth into a silver world like our Moon.'

So the Caribs descended to earth on their cloud chariots. As they drew near they marvelled at the bleakness of the towering peaks and at the thickness of the haze resting like a grey carpet on the plains and pastureland. 'We have much work to do,' said the oldest Carib. 'This haze has been getting thicker and darker year after year.'

Since there was so much to do, the Caribs divided up the work. The younger ones rubbed away the grey haze that carpeted the plains until the green glistened with light and the streams were full of sparkling radiance. The women scrubbed away the haze and gloom that veiled the valleys and the rising ground, scouring away the darkness from the flowers and leaves till they danced with light. The men burnished the higher ground and the grey mountain ranges, polishing them until the high peaks glowed with the fires of sunrise. So the first people, the Caribs, gave to the earth the three splendours that they knew, starlight, moonlight, and sunlight, filling the earth with sparkling radiance.

Their work accomplished, it was time to return. Also, the supply of food that they had brought with them was finished. But while the Caribs were working, their cloud chariots had broken loose and disappeared. Fear filled their hearts.

'Kabo Tano will hear us,' said the oldest Carib. 'Cry out to him.'

For a day and a night the Caribs called to Kabo

8

Tano, their voices rising and falling through the forest like the murmur of a distant stream. Then all was silence. No word came in reply. Kabo Tano gave them no sign, no far-off voice of thunder nor even the whisper of leaves stirring in the near-by forest. They were alone.

Through spreading savannah and steaming forest the Caribs wandered in search of food, for they were dying from hunger. In their distress they made cakes of red clay and baked them over a fire of coals, but Kabo Tano was not there to change the red clay into bread.

Then suddenly a young Carib, keener of eye than his fellows, pointed to a tall tree—and hope sprang up within them, for the branches of the tree were heavy with red berries which flocks of birds were eating. The Caribs hurried to the tree, tasted the berries and found them good. For a while the berries satisfied their craving for food, but the red juice held no nourishment for their wasting bodies. The children grew weak, women stumbled as they made their way across the savannah, and even the young men walked with dragging feet.

'Oh, that we had never left our home in the land of the Moon,' cried the Caribs in their distress.

Kabo Tano heard them. Seeing their weakness and misery he created for their comfort a mighty tree such as had not been before, each branch as huge as a forest tree, each heavy with fruit: this with oranges of rich gold, that with bunches of bananas ripening to a greenish yellow; here sapodillas ready for eating, there mangoes—with every kind of fruit growing and ripening on its own branch; and beneath the shadow of the tree grew all manner of plants that bear food: cassava, potatoes, yams, maize, and the like.

Mapuri the wild pig first found the tree, which was hidden in the depths of the forest. Thrusting his stubby nose through the thick grass and rooting about he came upon fruit that had fallen from the branches of the tree, and he found also the swelling roots of cassava and the potatoes hidden in the earth. Soon Mapuri, who had been as thin as a rake, grew sleek and fat. The Caribs

saw the change in the wild pig and wondered how it was that Mapuri grew fat while they faded away into shadows. They tried to follow Mapuri, but he heard them and hid in the long grass.

Then the oldest Carib said, 'We need help. Perhaps one of the animals will help us to track down Mapuri.'

'Perhaps the woodpecker,' said another. 'He can watch Mapuri from above and mark out the path he takes. Mapuri hears the noise of our footsteps on the earth, but he will not hear Woodpecker flying above him.'

So the Caribs sought out Woodpecker, and told him how the famished wild pig had grown heavy with fat. If Woodpecker could find out where Mapuri got his food he should have his share and the Caribs theirs.

Next morning Woodpecker set out, a good-hearted bird but stupid. He flew above the trees, watching Mapuri thrusting through the thick grass below, marking his track; but every now and then the bird perched on an old tree and tapped on its trunk. Mapuri heard the tapping. He noticed that, as he went farther into the forest, the tapping followed him. When he paused, the tapping stopped. He decided that Woodpecker was following him, and so hid himself until evening, when Woodpecker had to return home.

Disappointed, the Caribs sought out the most timid of all animals, Rat; for he, being timid, moved so softly and with such care, and was so skilled in hunting, so expert in remaining hidden, that Mapuri would not notice him.

Unseen, noiselessly, Rat followed Mapuri, who moved carefully, listening for Woodpecker, unaware that he had a companion. Reassured by the fact that there was no tapping, Mapuri moved quickly to his tree, and so Rat discovered the wild pig's secret. How good was the fruit, how satisfying the food, and how tasty. The mangoes swinging from the branches were full of rich yellow juice, the yams in the ground of the most delicate flavour, the plantains and bananas sweet and satisfying. This treasure of food was much too good to share with the starving Caribs, thought Rat! Besides, there were so many of them, and they were so hungry that the food, though plentiful, could not serve them all. So towards evening, Rat, having eaten, returned to those who had sent him, claiming that Mapuri had eluded him.

Certainly Rat seemed no stouter than when he set out, and the Caribs accepted his word, arranging that he should try again the following day. For a week Rat went off each morning, and returned each evening with a story of failure—of how Mapuri had got away from him by swimming across a stream, or had seemed suddenly suspicious and lain still all day. But the Caribs noted that Rat was beginning to put on weight. His ribs no longer stuck out. He seemed heavier and a little slower. At last, one evening, a Carib who was keener of eye than all the rest, saw scraps of food sticking to Rat's whiskers. He pointed this out to the others, and Rat for all his cunning had to tell the truth. Even then the Caribs would not trust him. One held Rat fast while he led the Caribs to the tree. At the sight of its branches heavy with fruit and the many crops flourishing in its shadow, the tribe sang a song of praise to Kabo Tano. The words echoed through the forest: 'Praise to Kabo Tano, the Ancient One, who gives us this precious tree.'

At that moment, to their astonishment, a voice came to the Caribs from far away, saying, 'Cut down the tree.'

In wonderment the men set about felling the tree with their stone axes. For ten months they laboured. At the end of the tenth month the Coomacka-Tree, swaying and groaning, fell with a sound like thunder. Each man took cuttings from the branches, trunk, and roots; and so, to this day, every Carib has food close to his dwelling.

The Crested Curassow

THE Caribs made their first home on earth in the savannahs and forests of Guyana. Some fashioned boats from the forest trees and set off down the great rivers to the coast and sea. Others stayed where they were, setting up shelters against the heat of the sun and the floods that sometimes descended on them from the heavens. Others journeyed for many nights to find what lay beyond the place where the mountains and the sky met each other. Each party of Caribs had its leader. Those who planted and made houses had a chief whom they chose, and likewise those who set off down the rivers and those who journeyed inland.

But the animals had no leader. They lived in the forest at the foot of Mount Roraima: Mapuri the wild pig, the parrot, the chattering monkey, the small powis bird, the jaguar with his soft tread and eyes that burned with yellow-green flame, the giant sloth, the toco toucan with a curving beak as long as his body. And because they had no leader every animal argued and squabbled and quarrelled with every other animal. Mapuri grew tired of the noise and confusion, and even the chattering monkey wished for silence.

At last the animals came together to choose a leader who would put an end to their quarrelling. They assembled in a clearing in the forest that flows like a dark, green sea around Mount Roraima, Red Mountain. So high is the peak that clouds wrap their soft folds around it, hiding it from sight; but its steep side glows pink at sunrise and sunset as if with a warm light of its own.

This lonely place should have been quiet, for there was no Carib near at hand to trap or hunt down the animals. But there was no peace. As the assemblage of animals grew larger the din and confusion increased. The screeching of flame-coloured and turquoise parrots, the chatter of the nimble brown monkey Irraweka, the scream of the toucan and the terrifying cry of the jaguar echoed through the forest, rising to the hidden peak of Mount Roraima itself. There was so much noise that at last even the noisiest animal grew tired and listened while Wise Owl said:

'We must have a leader. We must have a leader to be our judge, to settle our quarrels and keep peace among us.'

At these words the brown monkey Irraweka stood up and offered to be leader. He said that he knew all the best places in the forest; he knew where to find water and food. No other animal knew the forest as well as he did, for he spent his days swinging from one tree to another, leaping among the branches of even the mighty

Coomacka-Tree. But the other animals knew Irraweka
well. There was no animal in the forest so full of mischief, so quick to quarrel. They shouted him down.
They would not have him for leader.

Now Parrot, who had been watching from the branch
of a tree, flew down into the circle of animals and said
that he would be leader. What other bird had feathers
of such bright yellow and green, of such rich blue? And
who knew better where the most juicy berries and nuts
were to be found? He would be leader.

But the animals knew Parrot as well as they knew the
monkey Irraweka. They knew that he talked too much,
making speeches throughout the day, screeching and
screaming even when there was no one near.

So animal after animal offered to be leader. Mapuri
the wild pig was too selfish, seeking food only for himself and never thinking of others. The giant sloth was
kindly but far too lazy to be leader, and he might even
turn everything upside-down, for that was the way he
spent most of his time, fast asleep upside-down, clinging
to the branch of a tree.

For two days this went on, each animal offering to be
leader and all the others objecting. At last, on the third
morning, Wise Owl, who had been silent, looked up
and saw that the small powis bird was taking no part in
the argument. He sat by himself a little way off, listening
and keeping quiet.

'You want a leader, do you?' asked Wise Owl. Then
he said, 'That is easily settled. There is your leader,' and
he pointed to the powis bird.

'No, no,' cried the powis bird. 'I do not want to be
leader. Indeed, I cannot be leader for I have no voice.

My whistle is little more than a wretched croak. Oh no, Wise Owl, I cannot be leader.'

'Oh yes you can,' replied the Owl; 'for he who has a still tongue has a wise head.'

'True,' mumbled the giant sloth, who was hanging from a branch half-asleep. 'And if you haven't got much of a voice you will not be able to talk too much.'

'That is true,' said the jaguar, looking at Irraweka with his burning eyes. 'Yes, you won't chatter too much. You are our leader, powis bird.'

So, by the consent of all the animals at their great convention in the forest at the foot of the lonely Roraima, the quiet, grey powis bird was made leader.

Every day in that quiet hour before the light of the sun leaves the earth and the clouds come together more thickly on Roraima's peak, the birds and the animals of the forest met together under the shade of a mighty tree. They recounted the happenings of the day. Monkey chattered excitedly about the many things he had seen from the topmost branches of the forest trees, and Ant whispered of the many things that he had seen while crawling close to the earth. The strong and the weak, the large and the small sat together, and if there had been a quarrel among them the powis heard both sides and settled the matter.

Yet neither the powis nor his wife was happy. The powis felt that his whistle was too weak, too much like a feeble croak, and not impressive enough for the leader of all the animals. It worried him that when he had to settle a quarrel between the fierce tree-cat and the macaw with its flashing bright colours, he could not speak in a loud clear voice but only in a feeble whisper.

At last one evening, after a long day of worry, the powis
said to his Council of Animals:

'I have nothing which shows that I am your leader.'

'That's soon settled,' said Wise Owl. 'We will make
you a fine crest.'

In a moment the birds and animals were busy making
a crest for the powis. How beautiful it was when
finished. With its vivid feathers it seemed full of bright
jewels. It suited the powis perfectly, so perfectly that it
seemed always to have been there. He looked like a
king, so fine was his new crest.

'Hail, Powis,' cried the birds and the animals. 'Now
you are a crested bird. We must give you a new name,
one that suits your regal look.'

'No, no,' cried the powis in alarm; 'you cannot
change my name. If you do how will my family know
me?'

'That's easily settled,' said Wise Owl. 'We will give
you a new name and you can keep your old one. We
will call you Powis, which means the Teller of Tales,
but the world of men will call you the crested curassow.'

All the animals cheered and cried, 'Long live Powis
the crested curassow.'

Now it happened that next day all the animals went
about their business in the forest as was their custom;
the monkey to seek nuts, the parrot to hunt for bright
red peppers, the wild cow Abeyu to find the richest
patches of grass, the wild pig Mapuri to find the most
juicy roots. The powis went off to a tree where he knew
he would find berries for his wife and himself, while his
wife stayed behind to look after two lovely white eggs
in the nest.

The sun climbed up the cloudless sky and sent its hot rays searching through the forest, making a pattern of light through the branches and leaves. As the heat increased, Mrs. Powis grew thirsty, so thirsty that at last she left her nest and walked to a near-by stream to quench her thirst with the clear, cool water. Daintily she dipped her yellow beak into the running stream and drank her fill.

But while she drank there was a stir. A ripple broke the surface. She looked. Ah—there it was, a small, rainbow-coloured fish. The fish was her friend so she left it alone.

Near by were some shrubs and weeds. She went over to these and picked away at the seeds with her yellow beak. After she had satisfied her hunger she went back to her nest.

But, oh horror! Around the two lovely, gleaming white eggs a large snake had curled himself. She was terrified. She flapped her wings and flew off for help.

Abeyu the wild cow was feeding near by. Mrs. Powis flew to her and told her what had happened.

'Come along, I'll help you. I'll pierce him with my horns and crush him with my hoofs,' said Abeyu. But when they got near to the nest Mrs. Powis cried out:

'Oh, Abeyu, I don't think you can do any good. You

are so big that you will crush my eggs when you attack the snake.'

'That may well be,' said Abeyu sadly. 'Let us go and find someone smaller to help us.'

Off they hurried to where the wild pig Mapuri was digging for roots.

Mrs. Powis told Mapuri what had happened, and said, 'Come along and attack the snake.'

'Gladly,' cried Mapuri. 'Don't you know that a snake cannot live when I'm near by? I jump on to the snake's back and that's the end of him.'

'And that would be the end of my beautiful eggs, too,' cried Mrs. Powis, weeping bitterly. 'Oh, what shall I do?'

One animal after another offered to help. They all gathered round, but they were all too big. Then Wise Owl flew by and asked what was the matter. Weeping, Mrs. Powis told him her troubles.

'That's easily settled,' cried Wise Owl. 'We'll ask Ant to help us.'

'I'll gladly help,' said Ant, when he heard, 'and I will tell you how.'

'But you mustn't do anything that will make the snake thrash around and break my eggs,' cried the powis bird.

Ant whispered into Mrs. Powis's ear, telling her what he would do, and at last she was well content. Then he hurried away to fetch an army of ants. They marched quickly to the nest and with their sharp stings began to torment Snake. He would not have paid any attention to the sting of one ant, but with thousands of ants attacking him it was another matter. The pain soon became more than Snake could bear. He uncoiled his long body and hastily glided away to the water to cool his smarting skin. To this day he lives in the cool river, for fear of meeting another army of ants. He dare not come on to the land anywhere in the shadow of Mount Roraima whose steep side glows pink in the sunset; nor dare he come within the shade of the forest tree where the crested curassow lives, presiding over the Council of the Animals, with his wife beside him, and his two sons.

Irraweka, Mischief-maker

IN the beginning there was friendship between man and all the animals. The Caribs who made their homes on the red-earth terraces between the brown river and the dark forest did not fear the jaguar, nor did the jaguar crouch at the sight of man, yellow-green flame in his eyes, anger coursing through his tense body, motionless but for the nervous flick of the tip of his tail.

In those days men did not hunt down the wild pig, nor did Mapuri seek refuge when his sharp ears caught the sound of man's naked feet on the carpet of grass and leaves.

Many of the animals worked for man in those far-off days. Parrot, perched on the high branch of a tree, preening his gaudy feathers and blinking in the strong light, called out to the Carib sitting at the root of the tree, telling him the news of the world. The serpent went before man, showing him the quickest and easiest ways through the jungle. Dog and the great baboon and the giant sloth helped man, though often Sloth fell fast asleep in the middle of the work that he was doing. Even the restless, small brown monkey, Irraweka, gave man a hand.

And man helped the animals to find food. When, at Kabo Tano's command, he cut down the great tree and took cuttings from the trunk and branches, he did not forget the animals and their need. He knew that Mapuri felt thirst and hunger as he did, and the dog and jaguar, so he gave to all the animals pieces of the tree to plant as they wished, in the places where they dwelt.

But Irraweka hindered rather than helped, for he was always up to some trick. He pinched Mapuri the wild pig, pulled the tail of Abeyu the wild cow, shook the branch on which the parrot was balancing himself, leapt on the back of the jaguar dozing after lunch, and scolded Wise Owl for sleeping by daylight.

There came a time when Irraweka the mischief-maker nearly destroyed man and all the animals by interfering with man's work.

One day man went to the place where he had cut down the great tree and found a stream of water flowing fast from the root of the tree. Man was troubled, for the stream did not flow steadily like a river but swiftly, springing up as if it meant to cover the earth. To the rising water man said:

'O Stream, why are you flowing from the rest of the great tree, and why do you flow so swiftly?'

'I flow quickly because there is much to do,' replied the stream. 'Before the sun rises tomorrow I must cover the face of the earth.'

Terrified, man called out to the Ancient One, asking

him what to do. The Ancient One put it into man's
heart to make a large basket from the reeds that grew
near by, and to cover with this the hole from which
the water flowed. As soon as man placed the basket over
the hole the flow of water ceased, and he went away
content.

Now the brown monkey Irraweka saw man go into
the forest in the direction of the great tree and he followed him. He saw man making the basket, and he
watched from the far-off top of a cedar-tree while man
put the basket over the hole whence the water flowed,
but he was too far off to hear what man said. He thought
to himself: 'Man is our master but he does not think of
us. He keeps the best food for himself. He has hidden
the best fruit beneath the basket. When he goes I will
take away the basket and taste the food that man seeks
to keep for himself.'

After man had gone away, Irraweka removed the
basket. The stream flowed faster than ever. Soon it grew
into a river and then into a raging torrent that swept
away the terrified brown monkey, but not before the
other animals heard his cries. Parrot, perched aloft, saw
the water rising, saw Irraweka being swept away and
gave the alarm; and the animals cried out, 'O Man,
save us, save us.'

Man saw what was happening. He knew that he was
in peril and all the animals with him, so he led them to
the top of a high hill, on which grew coconut-trees, tall
and deeply rooted.

'Climb the coconut-trees,' cried man. 'Climb the
trees quickly before the flood sweeps you away.'

For five days all the animals and man lived in the

top of the coconut-trees, where the green branches spring from the trunk and the nuts grow. The rain fell, and the water rose until no land could be seen. The sky was blanketed with dark clouds, and thick mist hid the world.

Now a strange thing happened. While the flood was rising, all the animals were frightened, and man also, but the baboon was more terrified than any other animal. In those days his voice was shrill, his throat small; but at the sound of the rising water lapping around the trunk of the coconut-tree his shrill cries became hoarse shouts, his shouting became a loud roaring, and his throat grew to twice its former size. To this day all baboons have huge throats and the loudest voices in the forest.

Of a sudden, on the fifth night, there came stillness. The thunder and the lightning ceased. The rain stopped. The animals began to move from their places of refuge among the boughs of the coconut-trees, but man bade them stay where they were, saying that they should wait until the day dawned. On the morning of the tenth day the sun rose, but mist still covered the earth, and from below the trees came the sound of lapping water. Man dropped a coconut, and listened. In a moment there was a great splash. The animals knew that the water was still high.

Each day man dropped a coconut and all the animals listened. At first, the sound of splashing was close below them. Two days later it seemed more distant. On the following day there was no sound of splashing, only a dull thud. The listening animals eagerly made ready to climb down from the trees, but man told them to stay where they were. He would climb down first to make sure that all was safe.

The trumpeter bird did not do as man bade. Tired of sitting on the boughs of the coconut-tree, and proud of his long legs, he climbed down, while man shouted to him, 'Be careful, be careful, come back; you do not know what lies below.'

The trumpeter bird paid no heed. Climbing down quickly, he stepped into a nest of large ants that had buried themselves deep down within the earth while the rains were falling. Now they had come out of their hiding-place in search of food. Fierce with hunger, they bit at the long legs of the trumpeter bird, stripping the flesh from them before man could rescue the bird. To this day the trumpeter bird mourns because his legs are so thin.

Following after man, the other animals climbed down to the earth, sodden and cold. The toucan shivered so much that his long beak made music like a pair of castanets. Wise Owl shivered with cold for all his warm grey feathers. Mapuri the wild pig, who loves mud, found for once that there was too much mud for his pleasure and tried desperately to find a dry place.

While the animals were shivering with the cold, man began to make a fire. He found two sticks, rubbed them together until they grew hot, and so kindled a flame. Strangest of all was the fate that befell the alligator, a grumpy, quick-tempered animal, much disliked because he was so greedy. Alligator was proud of his long tongue, using it to sweep food into his mouth before any other animal could eat his fill. He went to pay his respects to man, hoping to get some food, for he was hungry. It was just after the marudi bird had swallowed the coal of fire, and man was angry because the labour of a morning had been lost and he must start all over again, rubbing two sticks together until he kindled a flame.

When the animals saw Alligator coming, they shouted, 'Perhaps he took the fire! Perhaps it was Alligator who stole your coal of fire, sweeping it into his mouth with his long tongue!' At these words man forced Alligator to open his mouth, and Alligator, in fear, swallowed half his tongue. To this day the alligator has a shorter tongue than any other animal.

These things happened because of Irraweka, mischief-maker. Up to this time all the animals had one language. They could speak to each other and to man. From this time of the great rains and the flood they grew fearful of each other, and each animal refused to speak to any other but his own kind. The birds chirruped and sang to each other, the baboon roared to his mate, the parrot screeched and laughed in his own language, the wild cow Abeyu lowed, the wild pig Mapuri grunted, the jaguar snarled, and the wise owl hooted as he flew through the dusk on flapping wings. Because Irraweka removed the basket from the fast-flowing spring at the root of the great tree, man and the animals no longer understood each other.

The Jaguar and the Crested Curassow

IN the confusion that followed the flood, the jaguar
was the first animal to go off by himself. Mapuri and
the wild cow Abeyu and the mischievous brown
monkey Irraweka joined the other animals in a circle
around the crested curassow every evening when the
sun dipped below the line of the forest on the distant
horizon and the shadow of Mount Roraima fell over the
land. Sometimes, once a week perhaps, the jaguar came,
but clearly he paid little heed to the crested curassow.
After all, he had claws of shining steel while the crested
curassow had thin, fragile feet. His roar echoed through
the forest, but the birds in the circle had to listen carefully to catch the hoarse words of the curassow. His
body was rippling muscle whereas the crested curassow
was a handful of feathers.

But Mapuri, Abeyu, and Irraweka liked to listen to
the tales of the crested curassow. Mapuri would say,
'Look, Abeyu, the shadow of Roraima begins to fall

over the forest. It is time to sit and talk with the crested curassow.'

'Yes,' nodded Abeyu. 'The little powis bird, our crested curassow, must be waiting for us. He is small in body, that bird, but large in mind.'

'And Wise Owl will be waiting,' said Mapuri, 'and restless Irraweka, and all except the jaguar.'

'Ah, Mapuri,' replied Abeyu, 'so you have seen what is happening. You know,' and here Abeyu shook her head violently, 'Jaguar needs a lesson.'

'But who can teach Jaguar a lesson?' asked Mapuri, looking at the distant peak of Roraima, rose-pink in the sunset. 'Jaguar is strong. Have you seen the muscles rippling through his body, or observed the sharpness of his teeth, or noticed the cruel claws that he sometimes unsheathes? Jaguar is strong, stronger than his fierce cousin the tree-cat, far stronger than any of us.'

Mapuri the wild pig and Abeyu the wild cow trotted off to the hathi-tree where the powis and the other animals were waiting for them. The jaguar was there also, but he looked angry. Mapuri and Abeyu knew the signs: the flick of Jaguar's restless tail, the fierce flash of his eye, the coiled tenseness of his body. This evening of all evenings Jaguar had no wish to stay and listen to tales under the hathi-tree. He had no wish to stay at home. The forest called him. Perhaps tonight he would find a fat calf drinking by a stream or a deer far from its home. He snarled so fiercely that the bright-eyed parrot almost fell from his perch on a branch of the hathi-tree.

'I will not stay here any longer,' snarled the jaguar. 'Give me strong meat, not these silly tales. If you tell us stories, tell how once I leaped on to the back of Mapuri's fat uncle, sank my claws in him, and put an end to him.' Jaguar looked at Mapuri, baring his teeth as if he were about to attack him. 'Or tell how I waited in the forest until Abeyu's stout father came along; he was a fine kill! I dragged his body half a mile into the depths of the jungle, and hid it among the bushes where no one else would find it. Ah, it was good!' Jaguar licked his lips with his red tongue.

Mapuri's small eyes burned with anger, Abeyu lifted her head sharply so that her horns stabbed the darkness; but what could Mapuri or Abeyu do? The jaguar was too strong.

Just then, Mapuri, Abeyu, and all the animals saw the crested curassow lift his head and look for a moment at the jaguar. There was no fear in the eyes of the powis bird. His voice was quiet, his manner calm as he said:

'Quite so, quite so. It's the time of evening when you like to kill. But before you go, Jaguar, pray that the fate which befell Kikushie may not overtake you.'

The jaguar was on the point of bounding away, his back arched for the leap. He paused and looked back, his eyes burning with hidden flames of green and yellow, and asked:

'Kikushie? Who was Kikushie?'

'Oh, surely you remember that Kikushie was an ancestor of yours?' replied the crested curassow quietly.

'Yes,' said Wise Owl, 'I remember Kikushie. Jaguar, . perhaps it would be well to do what the crested curassow says.'

'By all means go if you wish,' said the curassow

calmly. 'Off to the forest, where you may come upon one of Mapuri's kinsmen, or perhaps find one of Abeyu's brothers by the stream, or some gentle deer; but while you bound through the forest with noiseless strides, remember Kikushie.'

'Kikushie? I don't know anything about a relative with that name. What happened to Kikushie?'

'Sit and I will tell you,' said the curassow. 'How can I tell you while you stand there flicking your tail, your body tense? If you sit quietly I will tell you the story of Kikushie.'

In a bad temper, the jaguar sat. Mapuri stole a glance at Abeyu. Their eyes met for a moment. Perhaps, after all, the little crested currasow could teach Jaguar a lesson.

'Of course,' began the curassow, 'the story I am going to tell was told to me many years ago by my grandfather. He heard the tale from his grandfather; yet I think I can remember it all clearly.'

Jaguar flicked his tail restlessly. Mapuri, looking at him, could almost hear him saying, 'This silly, tiresome powis with his talk about grandfathers, when I wish to hear about Kikushie and then be away!' He could hardly restrain himself as the scent of the deep, dark forest came to his nostrils; but the quietness of the crested curassow held him.

'A long way from the shadow of Roraima,' said the curassow, 'a far journey away by boat, there is a mountain nearly as lofty as Roraima yonder. It is called Watipu. In the forests round about Watipu there is fine hunting. Yet the animals who lived in this lovely place were afraid. Kikushie, a fierce jaguar, lived in a cave high on the side of the mountain. At evening he hunted for dogs, deer, and wild pigs, even for Caribs. He would lie in wait for a man who had been overtaken by darkness and kill him. As for the dogs, the wild pigs and the wild cows, they all lived in constant fear of him.

'Kikushie's mate lived with him. One night he said to her:

"You go hunting tonight. I am tired. But do you know where to go? I saw a Carib lead a nice fat deer to his village and tie it in his compound. A piece of venison would make us a fine dinner."

'"I'll do my best," said Kikushie's mate, and she bounded away into the forest. She did not come back. She was not as cunning a hunter as Kikushie, nor was she as careful. The Caribs who were watching by the fire saw her dark shape as she stole through the bush towards them, and they shot her.

'After this Kikushie became fiercer than ever. He guessed what had happened. Evening after evening he raided the Carib villages, evading every trap they set, killing now a man, now an animal.

'At last the Caribs called a Council of War. "This cannot go on," they cried. "We must put an end to Kikushie so that we may sleep in peace. Our homes and our children are in constant peril. We must put our heads together and make a plan."

'"Just so," said the Carib chief. "I have an idea. We poison our creeks to catch fish. Let us poison our arrows and go to Kikushie's cave. He must come out at some time and then we will let fly our arrows at him."

'This was agreed. Three hundred Carib warriors armed themselves with bows and arrows and took with them the dreaded blowpipe with poison darts in it. On a night soon after the full moon, a time when the jaguar likes to go hunting, they surrounded the cave and waited.

'All was quiet, save that there was a gentle breath of wind in the forest and the distant murmur of a small

stream. Then the moon swung up above the tree-tops and at the same moment Kikushie left his cave. He was a magnificent sight. When the scent of the Caribs reached him he arched his back, bared his teeth and snarled. It was terrifying, but the Caribs held their ground.

'"Now," shouted the Chief. The arrows whistled through the air and Kikushie sank to the ground. How the Caribs rejoiced. They had freed their wives and children from terror. In the days that followed they painted some figures in red on the rocks of the cave, to tell the story of what they had done, and each Carib took up a stone and put it in a line with the others to mark the place.'

'To this day, O Jaguar,' said the curassow, 'you will find at the foot of the Watipu mountain a row of small white rocks placed close together, about fifty yards long. They mark Kikushie's grave.'

The crested curassow turned his head towards the jaguar.

'Well, off you go, Jaguar,' he said.

'No,' snarled the jaguar. 'I'll stay here.'

Mapuri and Abeyu looked at each other. Their eyes met. Mapuri winked slowly at Abeyu; Abeyu smiled at Mapuri.

The Dog's Nose is Cold

MAN went short of food during the months that followed the flood. Every morning he looked across at the cloud-covered face of Mount Roraima and prayed to Arawidi the sun-spirit to pierce the thick cloud and set the pink rocks burning with light. As he laid out his patch of cassava he prayed to the sun-spirit to warm the earth and make the roots swell to bursting.

It was at this time that man first became a hunter. Hungry, craving for food, he searched for wild honey, but the bees were not making honey because the flood had destroyed the flowers. Nor did man find fruits on the trees; there were no sapodillas, mangoes, not even the tart wild tamarind, for the flood had destroyed them. Finding no fruit, man set snares in the grass for birds that made their nests on the earth, and he made a bow and arrows with which to shoot the iguana, armadillo, and the wild pig, Mapuri. Choosing the toughest, longest canes that grew by the river, he made blow-pipes for shooting the animals, and he provided himself with spears by tipping the end of some reeds with sharp pieces of shell, bone, or flint.

Armed with spear, blowpipe, and bow and arrows, man went into the forest, but he was unskilled in the use of the weapons so that the spear he threw at Mapuri did no harm. The tip of bone buried itself in the bark of a mora-tree while the tough reed splintered. The arrow that he aimed at Woodpecker went wide of its mark, and was lost in a tangle of thorn-bushes. The blowpipe was too short, the darts that he shot through it travelling but a short distance. Man returned from the forest empty-handed, arrows spent, spear broken, blowpipe useless.

And the animals were no longer his friends. The woodpecker told how man had tried to kill him, Mapuri reported at the Council of Animals that man had thrown a sharp spear at him, and the armadillo told of the blowpipe and its darts. Word went round the forest: 'Man is a hunter. Keep out of his way.' The crested curassow forbade Parrot to give man news of the happenings in the forest world, and ordered the bell-bird to warn of man's approach. From that time, whenever man entered the forest the bell-bird warned all the animals with a slow tolling 'kong, kong, kong' like notes struck slowly on an anvil. If man came to-wards them he uttered a sharp 'qua-ting, qua-ting'. When man left the forest he told the other animals with a gentle, high-pitched 'kong-kay, kong-kay'.

Now, man the hunter was alone. No animal showed him friendship. Early one morning in the dry season, when from afar off he could see streams falling like white ribbons over the glowing rock face of Roraima, he went into the forest to seek a friend among the animals, leaving behind him his bow and arrows, his spear, and blowpipe. He would have a word with one of his old friends—Woodpecker, perhaps; or talkative Parrot who used to tell him the news of the world; or Mapuri; or even the chattering mischief-maker Irraweka, who often used to keep him company along the forest tracks, chattering, suddenly breaking off to chase a salamander up a tree, disappearing in search of nuts, then startling him by suddenly leaping out of the bush behind him. Troublesome Irraweka had been his friend; and man longed again for his companionship.

Standing still at the edge of the forest, man was hopeful, for he could hear the singing of the birds, parrots screaming at the tops of their voices, a macaw's shrill cry, the distant lowing of Abeyu talking to her calf. As soon as he entered the forest silence fell, the chatter and gossip of the animals ceased; all was quiet but for a slow 'kong, kong, kong' as if one were striking an anvil slowly; and as he went farther into the forest he heard a sharp 'qua-ting, qua-ting'. After this, man heard only his own breathing, the sound of the fallen leaves under his feet on the forest floor, the beating of his heart; and with these occasionally a stabbing 'qua-ting, qua-ting'.

And although man could not see them, he felt eyes fixed on him: the cold eyes of the snake, the fierce red eyes of the baboon, the burning yellow eyes of the jaguar. He knew that eyes were watching him through the green wall of the forest, not the eyes of friends, not eyes full of mischief, but the eyes of animals that were hunters like himself. Turning back from the fear and peril of the dark forest he went out into the sunlight to pray to the sun-spirit Arawidi for a friend, for one animal that would be his companion by day and guard by night, so sharp-eyed as to see the jaguar's track from a distance, so keen of smell as to pick up the armadillo's scent. Leaving the forest he heard, softly uttered, the two notes of a bird: 'kong-kay, kong-kay.'

Man knew that it was not safe for him to return to the forest without a friend. Each morning he looked towards the glowing face of Roraima, and up at the sky, the home of Arawidi. He prayed for an animal that would be his friend; then, in search of food for the day, he went down to the river to catch fish. Sitting on a log, his feet in the brown water, he pushed off from shore, but there were piranha in the river with teeth like razors, so in place of a log he made a raft of light branches; then, seeing how gracefully the long narrow seed-pods from a near-by tree floated, he made himself a canoe shaped like the seed-pod. Sitting in this he fished in the middle of a broad creek. Each evening smoke from a wood-fire rose in spirals above the trees surrounding the clearing where man roasted the fish he caught. Each morning the men of the tribe went out in their woodskin canoes. Each evening they returned laden with fish.

But the creek in which they were fishing was the favourite fishing-place of Arawidi the sun-spirit who sometimes appeared there in the shape of man. Arawidi saw that man was taking all the fish from the creek. At evening he saw the red glow of the wood-fire, and caught the smell of the burning wood and the fish, until at last he said to himself, 'If this goes on there will be no fish left in my creek. I will give man an animal as companion, to go with him into the forest, to help him find the hiding-place of the armadillo and the wild pig, and to keep watch over him at night. Then he will leave my creek and go back into the forest.'

That evening the sun-spirit, having finished his work in the sky, appeared as a man before the tribe seated around the wood-fire. On the ground lay the fish that the men had caught, of different sizes and colours. Arawidi took each fish in his hand in turn, moulded its body into the shape of the body of a dog, gave legs to the body, and moulded the head of the fish into the head of a dog; some with narrow foreheads, others with broad faces, just as dogs are to this day. The part of the head that Arawidi held in his hand became the nose, but it remained cold. So it is that to this day there is a dog in every Carib's home, watching over him at night, tracking down the animals for him when he goes hunting in the forest, living with him; and so it is also that every dog has a cold nose.

The Warau People Discover the Earth

THE Caribs were the first people on earth. After them came the Warau from a land beyond the sky, rich in birds of rare beauty but without animals of any kind. No deer grazed on its grassy plains, no jaguar roamed through its scattered woods, no fish swam in its clear, shallow streams. Instead there were large flocks of birds of rare beauty. Some of these the Warau killed for food; and each man made for himself from the feathers of the birds a richly coloured head-dress for wearing at great festivals.

One day while a young Warau hunter, Okonorote, was wandering through the fields he saw a bird more beautiful than any he had ever seen. In flight it was an exquisite jewel, the scarlet of its feathers more brilliant than those of the scarlet ibis, its green more vivid than the emerald feathers of the humming-bird. Enchanted by its rainbow loveliness, Okonorote swore not to return home until he had taken the bird. 'How splendid a head-dress these feathers will make,' he said to himself; 'lovelier than any fashioned in ancient times. These feathers will give joy to many. I must have them.'

For five days Okonorote followed the bird, using all his skill to come within bowshot while it settled to a meal of berries on some lofty branch. He crept towards the bird through the long grass, keeping out of sight, crawling, inching his way forward, holding his breath lest even that faint sound of breathing should startle it. Almost within range, he lifted the bow, put the arrow in place, then moved forward so gently that neither stirring of grass nor rustle of leaves told of his presence. Suddenly, even while he was pointing the arrow, the bird flew away and the pursuit began anew.

On the afternoon of the fifth day the bird settled on the low branch of a tree. Okonorote moved forward very slowly, making no sound. He kept his eyes fixed on the bird. His heart beat fast, for now he was nearer to it than he had ever been. He marvelled at the proud curve of the neck, the splendid crest of red and blue feathers, the rich hues of the rainbow plumage. He loosed his arrow. At that moment the bird flew up into the air. But it was too late. The arrow pierced the body. The bird fell back lifeless into the high grass.

Okonorote raced towards the place where the bird had fallen, shouting for joy. For five days he had watched, moving with care, making no sound, thinking only of the bird. Now he could throw caution to the winds. He raced at full speed towards the bird he had sought for so long. But it was not there. He thrust aside the dagger-points of the thorn-bush, the keen blades of the sword-grass and tore away the thick undergrowth covering the black swollen roots of the trees, but he could not find the bird. He had seen the arrow pierce its splendid body. He had seen it fall headlong into the thorn-bushes; but it was not there. Widening his circle of search, Okonorote came not to a gleaming bird but to a deep hole. Throwing himself face downward he looked over the edge of the hole, hoping to see the bird's body. To his astonishment he saw far below him a world of sunlit savannahs, green forests, and of animals grazing quietly—cattle, the fat, slow-moving tapir, and the swift deer.

With the skill of a hunter, Okonorote noted that the hole lay at the feet of a gentle hill, under the shelter of two cedar-trees that joined hands above it. Then he hurried back to tell of what he had seen, leaving signs to show the way: an arrow scratched on the bark of a mora-tree, a little heap of stones, a broken branch.

Many of the Warau people laughed at Okonorote's tale. Some said that he had fallen asleep and mistaken a dream for reality. The elders pointed out that for many years they had wandered far and wide through their land, and had never found this deep hole. Also, surely their fathers before them would have found it. After all, Okonorote was but a young man! Perhaps he had fallen into a hole hidden in the long grass and this had so shaken him that he was confused. Besides, no bird such as he described had been seen in their land. And even if Okonorote had seen such a bird, and he had put an arrow through it, how could it have vanished, leaving neither bones nor feathers?

A few of the young men, Okonorote's friends, believed him. They set off to find the hole, threw themselves face downwards beside it, and exclaimed in wonder at the beauty of the world below them, its sparkling streams, its forests, and, most wonderful of all, at the animals grazing on the savannahs.

'But how shall we get to that world?' asked the young men.

The wise men of the Waraus came together and talked, until at last one thought of a plan.

'Let us,' he said, 'make a long rope-ladder down which we can climb to this other world.'

'That will take many months,' said one.

'And who will be the first to climb down?' asked another.

'I will climb first,' replied Okonorote; 'for it may be that my bird lies on those savannahs that we can see. If I fail to return, only one man is lost. If I come back you will know that the way is safe.'

For many weeks the Warau girls and women picked cotton in the forest and wove it into a rope-ladder of great strength. This the men lowered through the deep hole, trying out the length of the rope. At the first trial it was too short. The women picked more cotton and lengthened the rope-ladder, but still it was too short. At the third trial it touched the trees in the forest far below.

As soon as the ladder had been made fast, Okonorote climbed down, descending first through the dark hole whose sides were smooth and damp, and then beyond towards the savannahs, the ladder swaying but holding fast; so, after half a day, he came to the trees, and finally, to the floor of the forest. Having tied the end of the rope-ladder firmly to a tree, he moved out on to the savannahs where the animals were grazing. He shot a young deer, kindled a fire, roasted the flesh and found it good. Packing up the rest of the meat, he climbed with it to his own land.

When the Waraus tasted the flesh of the deer they

longed for more. When Okonorote told them of the savannahs, forests, gleaming rivers, and high mountains, and above all of the deer and cattle, the tapir and the armadillo, they cried out, 'Let us go to this world below and see its wonders.'

So it came about that all the Warau people descended to the earth, climbing down the rope-ladder, passing first through the deep hole and coming at last to the forest. With Okonorote they searched for the bird, but there was no trace of it. Instead, they found guavas, pineapples, sapodillas, and bananas; and animals of many kinds.

Among the Warau people there was one only, a woman named Rainstorm, who did not like the earth. In the land above the sky she had been sad and lonely, keeping to herself, often full of tears. Because she often wept, her friends called her Rainstorm. On earth the forests and the savannahs gave her no pleasure, and the animals terrified her. After some months she decided to make her way back to the land above. But Rainstorm had grown fat on earth, and while she was climbing through the hole she stuck fast. Wedged tight, she could not move. There she remains to this day, wedged tightly in the hole, so that those who live on earth cannot see through the sky. And when clouds cover the sky and the rains begin to fall, the Warau people say, 'Rainstorm is weeping today.'

Tiger Story, Anansi Story

I. ANANSI ASKS A FAVOUR

ONCE upon a time, and a long, long time ago, all things were named after Tiger, for he was the strongest of all the animals, and King of the forest. The strong baboon, standing and smiting his chest like a drum, setting the trees ringing with his roars, respected Tiger and kept quiet before him. Even the brown monkey, so nimble and full of mischief, twisting the tail of the elephant, scampering about on the back of the sleeping alligator, pulling faces at the hippopotamus, even he was quiet before Tiger.

So, because Tiger ruled the forest, the lily whose flower bore red stripes was called tiger-lily, and the moth with broad, striped wings was called tiger-moth; and the stories that the animals told at evening in the forest were called Tiger Stories.

Of all the animals in the forest Anansi the spider was the weakest. One evening, looking up at Tiger, Anansi said:

'Tiger, you are very strong. Everyone is quiet in your presence. You are King of the forest. I am not strong. No one pays any attention to me. Will you grant me a favour, O Tiger?'

The other animals began to laugh. How silly of feeble Anansi to be asking a favour of Tiger! The bullfrog gurgled and hurried off to the pond to tell his wife how silly Anansi was. The green parrot in the tree called to her brother to fly across and see what was happening.

But Tiger said nothing. He did not seem to know that Anansi had spoken to him. He lay quiet, head lifted, eyes half closed. Only the tip of his tail moved.

Anansi bowed low so that his forehead almost touched the ground. He stood in front of Tiger, but a little to one side, and said:

'Good evening, Tiger. I have a favour to ask.'

Tiger opened his eyes and looked at Anansi. He flicked his tail and asked:

'What favour, Anansi?'

'Well,' replied Anansi in his strange, lisping voice, 'everything bears your name because you are strong. Nothing bears my name. Could something be called after me, Tiger? You have so many things named after you.'

'What would you like to bear your name?' asked Tiger, eyes half closed, tail moving slowly from side to side, his tawny, striped body quite still.

'The stories,' replied Anansi. 'Would you let them be called Anansi Stories?'

Now Tiger loved the stories, prizing them even more than the tiger-lily and the tiger-moth. 'Stupid Anansi,' he thought to himself. 'Does he really think that I am going to permit these stories to be called Anansi Stories, after the weakest of all the animals in the forest? Anansi Stories indeed!' He replied:

'Very well, Anansi. Have your wish, have your wish, but . . .'

Tiger fell silent. All the animals listened. What did Tiger mean, agreeing to Anansi's request and then saying 'but'? What trick was he up to? Parrot listened. Bullfrog stopped gurgling in order to catch the answer. Wise Owl, looking down from his hole in the trunk of a tree, waited for Tiger to speak.

'But what, Tiger? And it is so kind of you, Tiger, to do me this favour,' cried Anansi.

'But,' said Tiger, speaking loudly and slowly so that all might hear, 'you must first do me two favours. Two favours from the weak equal one favour from the strong. Isn't that right, Anansi?'

'What two favours?' asked Anansi.

'You must first catch me a gourd full of live bees, Anansi. That is the first favour I ask of you.'

At this all the animals laughed so loudly that Alligator came out of a near-by river to find out what was happening. How could weak Anansi catch a gourd full of bees? One or two sharp stings would put an end to that!

Anansi remained silent. Tiger went on, eyes half closed:

'And there is a second favour that I ask, Anansi.'

'What is that, Tiger?'

'Bring me Mr. Snake alive. Mr. Snake who lives down by the river, opposite the clump of bamboo-trees.

47

Both these things you must do within seven days, Anansi. Do these two small things for me, and I will agree that the stories might be called after you. It was this you asked, wasn't it, Anansi?'

'Yes, Tiger,' replied Anansi, 'and I will do these two favours for you, as you ask.'

'Good,' replied Tiger. 'I have often wished to sit and talk with Mr. Snake. I have often wished to have my own hive of bees, Anansi. I am sure you will do what I ask. Do these two little things and you can have the stories.'

Tiger leapt away suddenly through the forest, while the laughter of the animals rose in great waves of sound. How could Anansi catch live bees and a live snake? Anansi went off to his home, pursued by the laughter of Parrot and Bullfrog.

II. THE FIRST TASK: A GOURD FULL OF BEES

On Monday morning Anansi woke early. He went into the woods carrying an empty gourd, muttering to himself:

'I wonder how many it can hold? I wonder how many it can hold?'

Ant asked him why he was carrying an empty gourd and talking to himself, but Anansi did not reply. Later, he met Iguana.

'What are you doing with that empty gourd?' asked Iguana. Anansi did not answer. Still farther along the track he met a centipede walking along on his hundred legs.

'Why are you talking to yourself, Anansi?' asked Centipede, but Anansi made no reply.

Then Queen Bee flew by. She heard Centipede speaking to Anansi, and, full of curiosity, she asked:

'Anansi, why are you carrying that empty gourd? Why are you talking to yourself?'

'Oh, Queen Bee,' replied Anansi, 'I have made a bet with Tiger, but I fear that I am going to lose. He bet me that I could not tell him how many bees a gourd can hold. Queen Bee, what shall I tell him?'

'Tell him it's a silly bet,' replied Queen Bee.

'But you know how angry Tiger becomes, how quick-tempered he is,' pleaded Anansi. 'Surely you will help me?'

'I am not at all sure that I can,' said Queen Bee as she flew away. 'How can I help you when I do not know myself how many bees it takes to fill an empty gourd?'

Anansi went back home with the gourd. In the afternoon he returned to the forest, making for the logwood-trees, which at this time of the year were heavy with sweet-smelling yellow flowers and full of the sound of bees. As he went along he kept saying aloud:

'How many can it hold? How many can it hold?'

Centipede, who saw Anansi passing for the second time, told his friend Cricket that he was sure Anansi was out of his mind, for he was walking about in the forest asking himself the same question over and over again. Cricket sang the news to Bullfrog, and Bullfrog passed it on to Parrot, who reported it from his perch on the cedar-tree. Tiger heard and smiled to himself.

At about four o'clock that afternoon, Queen Bee, returning with her swarm of bees from the logwood-

49

trees, met Anansi. He was still talking to himself. Well
content with the work of the day, she took pity on him,
and called out:

'Wait there, Anansi. I have thought of a way of
helping you.'

'I am so glad, Queen Bee,' said Anansi, 'because I
have been asking myself the same question all day
and I cannot find the answer.'

'Well,' said Queen Bee, 'all you have to do is measure
one of my bees, then measure your empty gourd, divide
one into the other and you will have the answer.'

'But that's school-work, Queen Bee. I couldn't do
that. I was never quick in school. That's too hard for
me, too hard, Queen Bee. And that dreadful Tiger is so
quick-tempered. What am I to do, Queen Bee?'

'I will tell you how to get the answer,' said one of the
bees that advised the Queen. 'Really, it is quite easy.
Hold the gourd with the opening toward the sunlight
so that we can see it. We will fly in one at a time.
You count us as we go in. When the gourd is full we
will fly out. In this way you will find out the correct
answer.'

'Splendid,' said Queen Bee. 'What do you think of
that, Anansi?'

'Certainly that will give the answer,' replied Anansi,
'and it will be more correct than the school answer. It
is a good method, Queen Bee. See, I have the gourd
ready, with the opening to the sunlight. Ready?'

Slowly the bees flew in, their Queen leading the way,
with Anansi counting, 'One, two, three, four, five . . .
twenty-one, twenty-two, twenty-three . . . forty-one,
forty-two, forty-three, forty-four,' until the gourd was

half full, three-quarters full, '. . . a hundred and fifty-two, and fifty-three, and fifty-four.' At that point the last bee flew in, filling the gourd, now heavy with humming bees crowded together. Anansi corked up the opening and hurried off to the clearing in the forest where Tiger sat with a circle of animals.

'See, King Tiger,' he said, 'here is your gourd full of

bees, one hundred and fifty-four of them, all full of log-wood honey. Do you still want me to bring Brother Snake, or is this enough?'

Tiger was so angry that he could hardly restrain himself from leaping at Anansi and tearing him to pieces. He had been laughing with the other animals at Parrot's account of Anansi walking alone through the forest asking himself the same ridiculous question over and over. Tiger was pleased about one thing only, that he had set Anansi two tasks and not one. Well, he had brought the gourd full of bees. But one thing was certain. He could never bring Mr. Snake alive.

'What a good thing it is that I am so clever,' said Tiger to himself. 'If I had set him only one task I would have lost the stories.' Feeling more content within himself, and proud of his cleverness, he replied to Anansi, who was bowing low before him:

'Of course, Anansi. I set you one thing that I knew you could do, and one that I know you cannot do. It's Monday evening. You have until Saturday morning, so hurry off and be gone with you.'

The animals laughed while Anansi limped away. He always walked like that, resting more heavily on one leg than on the others. All laughed, except Wise Owl, looking down from his home in the cedar-tree. The strongest had set the weakest two tasks.

'Perhaps,' thought Owl to himself, 'perhaps . . . perhaps . . .'

III. THE SECOND TASK: MR. SNAKE

On Tuesday morning Anansi got up early. How was he to catch Mr. Snake? The question had been buzzing about in his head all night, like an angry wasp. How to catch Mr. Snake?

Perhaps he could trap Snake with some ripe bananas. He would make a Calaban beside the path that Snake used each day when the sky beat down on the forest and he went to the stream to quench his thirst. 'How good a thing it is,' thought Anansi, 'that Snake is a man of such fixed habits; he wakes up at the same hour each morning, goes for his drink of water at the same hour, hunts for his food every afternoon, goes to bed at sunset each day.'

Anansi worked hard making his Calaban to catch Snake. He took a vine, pliant yet strong, and made a noose in it. He spread grass and leaves over the vine to hide it. Inside the noose he placed two ripe bananas. When Snake touched the noose, Anansi would draw it tight. How angry Mr. Snake would be, to find that he had been trapped! Anansi smiled to himself while he put the finishing touches to the trap, then he hid himself in the bush by the side of the track, holding one end of the vine.

Anansi waited quietly. Not a leaf stirred. Lizard was asleep on the trunk of a tree opposite. Looking down the path Anansi could see heat waves rising from the parched ground.

There was Snake, his body moving quietly over the grass and dust, a long, gleaming ribbon marked in green and brown. Anansi waited. Snake saw the bananas and moved towards them. He lay across the vine and ate the bananas. Anansi pulled at the vine to tighten the noose, but Snake's body was too heavy. When he had eaten the bananas Snake went on his way to the stream.

That was on Tuesday. Anansi returned home, the question still buzzing about in his head: 'How to catch Snake? How to catch Snake?' When his wife asked him what he would like for supper, he answered, 'How to catch Snake?' When his son asked if he could go off for a game with his cousin, Anansi replied, 'How to catch Snake?'

A Slippery Hole! That was the answer. Early on Wednesday morning he hurried back to the path in the forest where he had waited for Snake the day before, taking with him a ripe avocado pear. Snake liked avocado pears better even than bananas. In the middle of the path Anansi dug a deep hole, and made the sides slippery with grease. At the bottom he put the pear. If Snake went down into the hole he would not be able to climb back up the slippery sides. Then Anansi hid in the bush.

At noon Snake came down the path. 'How long he is,' said Anansi to himself; 'long and strong. Will I ever be able to catch him?'

Snake glided down the path, moving effortlessly until he came to the Slippery Hole. He looked over the edge of the hole and saw the avocado pear at the bottom. Also he saw that the sides of the hole were slippery. First he wrapped his tail tightly round the trunk of a slender tree beside the track, then lowered his body and ate the avocado pear. When he had finished he pulled himself out of the hole by his tail and went on his way to the river. Anansi had lost the bananas; now he had lost the avocado pear also!

On Wednesday Anansi spent the morning working at a 'Fly-Up', a trap he had planned during the night while the question buzzed through his head: 'How to catch Snake. How? How?' He arranged it cleverly, fitting one of the slender young bamboo-trees with a noose, so that the bamboo flew up at the slightest touch, pulling the noose tight. Inside the noose he put an egg, the only one that he had left. It was precious to him, but he knew that Snake loved eggs even more than he

did. Then he waited behind the clump of bamboos.
Snake came down the path.

The Fly-Up did not catch Snake, who simply lowered
his head, took the egg up in his mouth without touching
the noose, and then enjoyed the egg in the shade of the
clump of bamboos while Anansi looked on. He had lost
the bananas and avocado pear, and his precious egg.

There was nothing more to do. The question 'How to
catch Snake?' no longer buzzed round and round in his
head, keeping him awake by night, troubling him
throughout the day. The Calaban, the Slippery Hole,
and the Fly-Up had failed. He would have to go back
to Tiger and confess that he could not catch Snake.
How Parrot would laugh, and Bullfrog and Monkey!

Friday came. Anansi did nothing. There was no more
that he could do.

Early on Saturday morning, before daybreak, Anansi
set off for a walk by the river, taking his cutlass with
him. He passed by the hole where Snake lived. Snake
was up early. He was looking towards the east, waiting
for the sun to rise, his head resting on the edge of his
hole, his long body hidden in the earth. Anansi had not
expected that Snake would be up so early. He had forgotten Snake's habit of rising early to see the dawn.
Remembering how he had tried to catch Snake, he
went by very quietly, limping a little, hoping that Snake
would not notice him. But Snake did.

'You there, you, Anansi, stop there!' called Snake.

'Good morning, Snake,' replied Anansi. 'How angry
you sound.'

'And angry I am,' said Snake. 'I have a good mind to
eat you for breakfast.' Snake pulled half his body out of

55

the hole. 'You have been trying to catch me. You set a
trap on Monday, a Calaban. Lizard told me. You
thought he was asleep on the trunk of the tree but he
was not; and as you know, we are of the same family.
And on Tuesday you set a Slippery Hole, and on
Wednesday a Fly-Up. I have a good mind to kill you,
Anansi.'

'Oh, Snake, I beg your pardon. I beg your pardon,'
cried the terrified Anansi. 'What you say is true. I did
try to catch you, but I failed. You are too clever for me.'

'And why did you try to catch me, Anansi?'

'I had a bet with Tiger. I told him you are the longest
animal in the world, longer even than that long
bamboo-tree by the side of the river.'

'Of course I am,' shouted Snake. 'Of course I am.
You haven't got to catch me to prove that. Of course I
am longer than the bamboo-tree!' At this, Snake, who
was now very angry and excited, drew his body out of
the hole and stretched himself out on the grass.' Look!'
he shouted. 'Look! How dare Tiger say that the
bamboo-tree is longer than I am!'

'Well,' said Anansi, 'you are very long, very long indeed. But Snake, now that I see you and the bamboo-
tree at the same time, it seems to me that the bamboo-
tree is a little longer than you are; just a few inches
longer, Snake, half a foot or a foot at the most. Oh,
Snake, I have lost my bet. Tiger wins!'

'Tiger, fiddlesticks!' shouted the enraged Snake.
'Anyone can see that the bamboo-tree is shorter than I
am. Cut it down you stupid creature! Put it beside me.
Measure the bamboo-tree against my body. You
haven't lost your bet, you have won.'

Anansi hurried off to the clump of bamboos, cut down the longest and trimmed off the branches.

'Now put it beside me,' shouted the impatient Snake.

Anansi put the long bamboo pole beside Snake. Then he said, 'Snake, you are very long, very long indeed. But we must go about this in the correct way. Perhaps when I run up to your head you will crawl up, and when I run down to see where your tail is you will wriggle down. How I wish I had someone to help me measure you with the bamboo!'

'Tie my tail to the bamboo,' said Snake, 'and get on with the job. You can see that I am longer!'

Anansi tied Snake's tail to one end of the bamboo. Running up to the other end, he called, 'Now stretch, Snake, stretch!'

Snake stretched as hard as he could. Turtle, hearing the shouting, came out of the river to see what was happening. A flock of white herons flew across the river, and joined in, shouting, 'Stretch, Snake, stretch.' It was more exciting than a race. Snake was stretching his body to its utmost, but the bamboo was some inches longer.

'Good,' cried Anansi. 'I will tie you round the middle, Snake, then you can try again. One more try, and you will prove you are longer than the bamboo.'

Anansi tied Snake to the bamboo, round the middle. Then he said:

'Now rest for five minutes. When I shout, "Stretch," then stretch as much as you can.'

'Yes,' said one of the herons. 'You have only six inches to stretch, Snake. You can do it.'

Snake rested for five minutes. Anansi shouted, 'Stretch.' Snake made a mighty effort. The herons and Turtle cheered Snake on. He shut his eyes for the last tremendous effort that would prove him longer than the bamboo.

'Hooray,' shouted the animals, 'you are winning, you are winning, four inches more, two inches more . . .'

At that moment Anansi tied Snake's head to the bamboo. The animals fell silent. There was Snake tied to the bamboo, ready to be taken to Tiger.

From that day the stories have been called Anansi Stories.

Tiger in the Forest, Anansi in the Web

For a time Anansi and Tiger were friends. Anansi liked to be with Tiger, who was strong, while Tiger was amused by the tricks that clever Anansi played on all the animals, using his wits to avoid doing any work, yet always managing to persuade Monkey or Hen, Dog or Puss to share their meals with him. When everyone was hard at work, Anansi watched from the shade of a tree, yet his bag of food was always full, and his wife and children had enough to eat.

In the hot season Anansi and Tiger went every day to the river for a swim. One day Tiger took with him a delicious stew that his wife had made, with large dumplings, thick gravy, and tender pieces of meat of the gibnut and accouri. This was Tiger's favourite dish and it was also a dish that Anansi could not resist. As the two friends strolled down to the river, Anansi kept his eyes on the large tin of stew. The smell made his mouth

59

water so that he could hardly talk; and he began to think of ways of getting the stew for himself.

'Let's try a new place for our swim, Tiger,' said Anansi; 'up by the rocks where there is a deep hole, so deep that everybody calls it the Blue Hole.'

'Very well,' replied Tiger. 'But do you think that you can swim there, Anansi? That is deep water.'

'You swim so well that I won't worry,' said Anansi. 'If I get into trouble I know you will help me, Tiger, for we are good friends. We share everything.'

'But I can't share my lunch with you today,' replied Tiger. 'This stew of accouri and gibnut is my favourite. My wife got the meat in the market and cooked it specially for me. You can smell how good it is, can't you, Anansi?'

'Yes, I can. Yes, I can. Yes, yes,' said Anansi with that strange, soft lisp of his. He pronounced 's' like 'sh', and spoke in a high-pitched voice. The smell of the stew was so tempting that he could not take his eyes off the tin.

At the Blue Hole, Anansi said, 'Brother Tiger, you are a big man, you go in and try out the water first. I will come in after you.'

Tiger replied, 'Very well, Brother Anansi. I will put the tin of stew where no one can trouble it, on this stump of an old cotton-tree. There I can keep my eyes on it. Then I will dive in. But you must come in when I call you. I am not going to leave you with that stew for long.'

'You go first, and try out the depth of the water,' said Anansi, 'and I will follow.'

Tiger dived in. Anansi shouted, 'Try out the deep,

deep parts, Tiger, where it looks blue-blue, yes, yes.'

Tiger loved swimming and diving. He took a deep breath and dived, trying to reach the sandy bottom of the river, but the water was deeper than he expected. He came up to the surface, looked round quickly to make sure that his stew was safe, took a deep breath, and dived again. While Tiger was under the water Anansi emptied the tin of stew on to a large green plantain leaf, put the tin back on the stump, and sat in the shade where Tiger could not see him. There he quickly ate the stew, while Tiger dived and swam. At last Tiger called out:

'Come in, Anansi, come in.' He could see the tin on the stump where he had left it. 'Ah,' he thought, 'soon I will have my lunch.' Then he shouted, 'You are a lazy fellow, Anansi. I am coming to throw you into the water!'

Anansi was very frightened. What would Tiger do when he found that the tin was empty? He called out:

'No, Tiger, no; I am frightened. I don't want to be thrown into the water. I am going back home.'

Anansi hurried to Big Monkey Town, which was only half a mile away. He said to Big Monkey, 'Brother Monkey, I was down at the Blue Hole with Tiger and I heard them sing a song (he said 'shing a shong') and this is how it went:

> *'This lunch-time I ate Tiger's stew,*
> *This lunch-time I ate Tiger's stew,*
> *This lunch-time I ate Tiger's stew*
> *But Tiger didn't know.'*

Big Monkey shouted at Anansi, 'What nonsense. Run away. Leave our town. We don't want to hear your silly song.'

Anansi hurried on to Little Monkey Town near by, where all the little monkeys lived, the small brown monkey, the marmoset, and the capuchin monkey. He said to them:

'Brer Monkey, I heard a sweet, sweet song down by the river, and this is what it said:

> *'This lunch-time I ate Tiger's stew,*
> *This lunch-time I ate Tiger's stew,*
> *This lunch-time I ate Tiger's stew*
> *But Tiger didn't know.'*

'That's a good dance-tune,' cried Capuchin Monkey, who loved nothing better than dancing, 'a very good dance-tune indeed. Let's learn it.'

All the little monkeys began to learn the song. They said to Anansi, 'Sing it slowly, so we can get the tune right.' Anansi sang the song over and over again until the little monkeys had learnt it. Then they said:

'Anansi, we will have a big dance tonight, and you must come back to hear us sing this song.'

That evening, when Anansi heard the little monkeys singing the song and dancing, he hurried off to Tiger, who was in a rage, questioning animal after animal about his lunch.

'Come with me, Tiger,' said Anansi, 'and you will find out what you want to know. Do you know what they are singing in Little Monkey Town? Listen.'

The sound of singing and music came faintly on the night wind. Anansi began to pick up the words of

the song as if they were new to him. 'I can't get it all,
Tiger, but it's something about eating Tiger's stew and
Tiger didn't know.'

Tiger and Anansi raced off to Little Monkey Town,
Tiger bounding along with great strides so that Anansi
could hardly keep up with him. Near the town, Anansi
said:

'Hide in the bush, Tiger, for we must make sure first.
Listen.'

The little monkeys were playing and singing and
dancing to the tune Anansi had taught them:

> *'This lunch-time I ate Tiger's stew*
> *But Tiger didn't know.'*

'Hear that, Tiger?' asked Anansi. 'Didn't I tell you?
Do you hear? Listen again. There it is—

> *'This lunch-time I ate Tiger's stew*
> *But Tiger didn't know.'*

'But I know now,' roared Tiger, breaking through
the bush into Little Monkey Town, with Anansi behind
him. He leaped through an open window into the
middle of the dance-hall and cried:

'So you ate my stew, did you?'

'What are you talking about?' asked one of the
little monkeys. 'We learnt that song from Anansi.'

Tiger was too enraged to listen. 'I am going to teach
you all a lesson,' he shouted, his teeth flashing in the
light.

Capuchin Monkey, the fastest runner of all, made

for Big Monkey Town at full speed to ask for help, while Tiger and Anansi began to attack the little monkeys, who were scattering in fright. Soon a troop of big monkeys arrived. At the sight of them Tiger took to the bush. He lives there to this day. Anansi, frightened almost out of his wits, climbed up into the top of the house. He lives there safe in his web, hiding from the monkeys.

Mancrow, Bird of Darkness

ONCE upon a time there was a bird in the forest that put all the world in darkness. Its name was Mancrow. Every animal feared Mancrow, and every man hated her, because she shut out the light. On the brightest day, with the sun shining from a cloudless sky, Mancrow cast a dark shadow over the forest, and the singing birds fell silent and the rabbits scurried into their holes.

In order to put an end to the darkness and to bring light back into the world, the King offered half his kingdom to anyone who killed Mancrow. 'He shall have half the treasure in my palace, half the diamonds and pearls, half the silver and gold; and I will give to him in marriage the loveliest of my three lovely daughters.'

Parties of hunters set off for the forest to kill Mancrow and bring light to the world. They found the tall tree in which Mancrow lived, but no man could kill the

65

bird. Soldiers from the King's army went out, but they all failed.

Now an old woman and her grandson lived on the edge of the forest, in a poor hut far from the King's palace. The name of the young man was Soliday. He was handsome and brave, but very poor. When he heard of the rewards that the King offered, Soliday, seeing how hard his grandmother had to work, cooking, washing clothes, and searching for wood in the forest, said:

'Grandmother, we are very poor and you have to work too hard. Tomorrow I will go into the forest to kill Mancrow.'

Soliday's grandmother replied:

'Grandson, you had better sleep here in safety. Do not venture into the forest to meet your death. You haven't even got a bow and arrow with which to shoot Mancrow.'

'Tomorrow I will go into the town,' said her grandson. 'Give me money to buy a bow and six arrows.'

'But what will you do with so many arrows?' asked the grandmother. 'I have very little money, perhaps not enough to buy six arrows. Look in that broken blue jar on the shelf and take whatever is in it. But be careful, Soliday.'

The money in the old jar was just enough to buy the bow and six arrows. On his return from the town with his bow and arrows, Soliday asked his grandmother to bake him six small cakes. Putting these in his knapsack he set off into the forest in search of Mancrow.

For three days Soliday searched until at last he came to a tall tree, the tallest in the forest. Mancrow sat on the topmost branch, dark against the sky.

At the sight of the bird that put all the world in darkness, Soliday sang:

> *'Good morning to you, Mancrow,*
> *Bird of darkness,*
> *Good morning to you, Mancrow,*
> *Bird of darkness*
> *You will die this bright morning.'*

In reply the bird sang:

> *'Good morning to you, Soliday,*
> *So far from home,*
> *What seek you, Soliday,*
> *So far from home?'*

'I seek you, Mancrow,' replied Soliday. He aimed his first arrow at Mancrow. Two of the bird's feathers fell to the ground, and Mancrow flew down from the topmost branch to the branch just below.

Again Soliday sang:

> *'Good morning to you, Mancrow,*
> *Bird of darkness,*
> *Good morning to you, Mancrow,*
> *Bird of darkness*
> *You will die this bright morning.'*

Mancrow replied:

> *'Good morning to you, Soliday,*
> *So far from home,*
> *What seek you, Soliday,*
> *So far from home?'*

67

As he had done the first time, Soliday answered, 'I seek you, Mancrow.' He shot his second arrow and two more feathers fell from Mancrow's wing. The bird flew down to the branch next below.

So the singing and the shooting went on, and each time that Soliday shot at the bird two feathers fell from Mancrow's wing. Five times Soliday shot at Mancrow, two feathers falling each time. Five arrows had pierced the bird, which was now sitting on the lowest branch of the tree.

Hidden behind the leaves on the branch of a mango-tree, Anansi watched what was happening. He heard Soliday sing his song. He saw him shoot his five arrows and saw the feathers fall from the bird's wing. He listened while Soliday sang his song for the sixth and last time,

heard Mancrow's reply, and watched while Soliday shot Mancrow with his last arrow. He saw the Bird of Darkness fall to the ground.

Soliday took up the bird, cut off its golden tongue and golden beak, put these in his knapsack, and went away in the direction of his cottage, leaving the bird on the ground.

Climbing down quickly from the mango-tree, Anansi picked up Mancrow and hurried off to the palace of the King. He knocked on the iron gate, rattling and pulling at it until the King himself, hearing the noise, looked through one of the palace windows and asked:

'Who is there? What is your name?'

'Mr. Anansi is my name,' came the reply.

'And what do you want, Mr. Anansi?'

'I am the man that killed Mancrow,' shouted Anansi.

'Admit Mr. Anansi immediately,' ordered the King. 'Give him fine clothes and all the money he wants. Tell my daughter, the loveliest of the three, to make herself ready for her wedding to Mr. Anansi.'

The soldiers of the guard let Anansi into the palace, and the King's servants, treating him with great honour as if he were the King's own son, dressed him in clothing of fine velvet and prepared a feast for him. They gave him the place of honour at the King's table, putting him in the centre, between the King and his daughter, but Anansi would not sit there. Instead, he chose a seat near the door where he could watch the palace gate. Half-way through the feast Anansi saw Soliday at the gate. 'Excuse me,' he said. 'I will soon be back,' and he went into one of the side-rooms, waiting to see what would happen.

Soliday knocked at the gate.

'What do you want?' asked the Captain on guard.

'I killed Mancrow,' answered Soliday.

'Impossible,' said the Captain of the Guard. 'Mr. Anansi killed Mancrow. He brought the bird's body here. He is eating with the King and the King's daughter. You had better go away.'

Soliday took from his knapsack Mancrow's golden tongue and beak of gold and asked:

'Can a bird live without tongue or beak?'

The soldiers of the guard looked at the bird's mouth and found that what Soliday said was true. They hurried into the King's room, reporting what they had found and seeking for Anansi to arrest him. They called:

'Come here, Anansi, the King wishes to speak with you.'

'I will soon be there,' replied Anansi from the side-room.

Again they called. Anansi answered, 'I do not feel very well, I do not feel very well.' While saying this, he was making a hiding-place among the shingles of the roof.

'Break the door down and bring Anansi here,' commanded the King.

The soldiers broke the door open and rushed into the room, but Anansi was nowhere to be found. He had hidden himself in the roof among the shingles.

Soliday married the King's daughter, and his old grandmother lived in the King's palace, but Anansi remains in the roof to this day.

Anansi and Snake the Postman

No one ever disliked work as much as Anansi did. While Hen worked hard, teaching her chickens how to scratch for food in the dust and gravel, Anansi rested under the shade of a mango-tree. While Monkey hunted through the forest for fruit and nuts, Anansi sat at his gate greeting those who passed by, asking this one to lend him a loaf of bread and that one to give him half a bunch of bananas.

Although Anansi liked to get letters, he disliked going to the Post Office for them, saying that the office was too far away. One day while he sat in front of his gate he saw Snake returning from the village with a letter. Snake moved with such smoothness and ease that Anansi called out to him:

'Mr. Snake, you move so quickly and easily that you would make the best postman in the whole world.'

Snake was very pleased at this, for he liked flattery. He replied, 'I am glad you think so, Anansi.'

'Yes, indeed,' said Anansi. 'And would you do me a favour, Snake? Would you be postman for me?'

'What do you mean?' asked Snake. 'What work would I have to do?'

'You would have to carry messages and take letters to the Post Office and go for the newspaper every morning. It's easy work, Snake. You move so quickly that you would do it all in half an hour or so.'

'But how much would you pay me?' asked Snake. 'I couldn't give up my time to do the work of postman for nothing.'

Anansi said:

'Snake, I know that you like the taste of blood. You can come to my home every night while I am asleep and bite me on the head. You mustn't bite too hard, Snake. I will let you do that if you will be my postman.'

What Anansi said about Snake was quite true. He loved the taste of blood and the prospect of biting fat Anansi on the head every night pleased him. Snake agreed to be postman. He turned up bright and early the following day to begin his work.

Anansi kept Snake busy throughout the day. He had to take a letter to the village, then return to get money to buy a stamp for the letter. Later, he had to go back to the village shop to ask the shopkeeper for half a pint of flour, and to the butcher's to borrow a pound of bone for making soup. Snake was up and down all day, carrying messages and doing errands for Anansi, but he comforted himself by remembering that he would bite Anansi on the head that evening.

Late that night Snake came to Anansi's house. Anansi was asleep, but he had left the door open, so

Snake entered and bit him. It was a sharp bite which
Anansi felt keenly. Snake was happy to taste blood, but
Anansi became troubled about his bargain. Next
day he kept Snake busy running to and from the
village, but he knew that he could not stand another
bite.

That evening Anansi invited his friend Rabbit to have
dinner and stay the night. Rabbit enjoyed his meal with
Anansi, but he became suspicious when Anansi insisted
on moving out of the room in which he usually slept
and giving up his bed. Rabbit knew that Anansi
was a selfish man, looking after his own comfort. He
said:

'My good friend Anansi, why are you giving up
your room to me? And your comfortable bed? You
stay here. I will sleep on the high bed in the other
room.'

Now Anansi could not pronounce the letter 'r' pro-
perly because of his lisp. Instead of 'Rabbit' he said
'Yabbit'. He replied, 'Oh, my dear, dear Yabbit, I
couldn't allow that at all, no, not at all. You must be
comfortable, my brother Yabbit. I will sleep in the
small room on that high bed. You stay here. Later in
the evening a cousin of mine will be coming here to
sleep. When you hear him call, just open the door and
see who it is.'

In those days there were no electric lights. Some
people used candles, but Anansi used a kerosene lamp.
Rabbit went to bed, and at eight o'clock Anansi put
out the lamp; but Rabbit could not sleep. He could not
understand why Anansi had given him that special
room and his own bed. After tossing restlessly for an

hour, he quietly dug a hole under the door and went off to his own home, where he soon fell asleep.

At eleven o'clock Snake arrived. He had worked hard all day as Anansi's postman, and had fallen asleep before dinner. Now he was refreshed, and ready for a taste of blood. Coming to the door of Anansi's room, he called out:

'Anansi, Anansi, open the door. Postman Snake is here!'

There was no reply. Anansi was sure that Rabbit would wake up and let Snake in, but no sound came from Rabbit. Snake called again and again. Rabbit made no reply. Anansi could not hear any stirring in the bed. He tiptoed to the door of Rabbit's room and called: 'Cousin Yabbit, Cousin Yabbit, wake up, wake up and open the door.'

Outside, Snake was calling angrily, 'Anansi, Anansi, it's Snake the postman.'

So the calling went on. Inside the house Anansi cried, 'Godfather Yabbit, Godfather Yabbit,' then again, 'Brother Yabbit, Brother Yabbit,' and finally, 'My Daddy Yabbit, my Daddy Yabbit.'

Outside, Snake, growing impatient, kept knocking on the door and shouting, 'Anansi, Anansi, Postman Snake is here! Postman Snake is here!'

Getting no answer, Anansi lit a lamp and went into Rabbit's room to rouse him. Instead of Rabbit he found a little pile of earth, and a hole under the door. Rabbit had gone.

What was Anansi to do? He liked having Snake as postman, but the first bite had hurt him far more than he had thought possible. Indeed, his head was still painful and sore. Rabbit had proved a false friend, and escaped before Snake exacted his day's pay. Anansi began to cry out and complain, telling Snake that his head hurt him, the bite had gone deep, he would have to go to the doctor, perhaps he would die from snake-bite!

Snake wanted blood. He had an answer for every-thing that Anansi said. If the first bite hurt, the second would not hurt as much and the third would hardly be noticed. At the thought of a third bite Anansi shuddered. And perhaps a fourth bite! How stupid he had been to have made this bargain with Snake!

Snake was growing angry. 'Open the door,' he cried. 'Open the door, Anansi, or I will bring a policeman here to make you keep your bargain.'

At that moment Anansi's eyes fell on a large, black iron pot standing by the stove. He snatched up the pot and put it over his head.

'Ready now, Snake,' he called. 'I am sorry to have held you up like this, but my head was hurting me. But I am ready now.'

Anansi put his head through the door, the pot pro-tecting it. In the darkness Snake did not see the pot. Angry at his hour of waiting, he struck at Anansi's head, biting as hard as he could. His teeth and lips struck the pot with such force that he cried out, then hurried away, his mouth bleeding and sore. Next day a messen-ger came to tell Anansi that Snake was giving up his job as postman, and that he was too ill to return that night for his wages.

How happy Anansi was at this news! He told the messenger to let Snake know that he also was ill in bed with a sore head: and as the messenger set off down the road, Anansi sang:

> '*Somebody waiting for Mr. Snake,*
> *But not Anansi,*
> *Somebody else can be postman,*
> *But not Snake, but not Snake!*'

Dry-Bone and Anansi

ONCE upon a time, and a long, long time ago, there was an old, old man, a skin-and-bone man whose name was Dry-Bone. He lived year after year, from the beginning of time to the year when the great earthquake shook the land and changed the shape of the Roraima mountain, and beyond that to the time when the great hurricane blew, stripping the coconuts from the trees, and blowing Dry-Bone far out to sea so that no one ever saw him again. Up to the time of the hurricane Dry-Bone was a terror to every hunter in the forest, for he had magic powers. The old skin-and-bone man could assume the shape of a bird, spreading his wings and taking pleasure in the sun's warmth. At other times he became a nimble deer, dancing and prancing through the open land by the stream.

But the hunter who shot the bird Dry-Bone or the deer Dry-Bone was in trouble for a long, long time. And Anansi was in great trouble on the day he met Dry-Bone, the skin-and-bone man.

77

Anansi should have known better, for while he was a small boy, not yet old enough to go to school, his mother Crooky had warned him about Dry-Bone, and had told him the story of Goat as a warning. Goat had never been the same after meeting Dry-Bone. This is how it happened.

Goat was a great hunter, and a boastful man, calling through the village in a loud voice whenever he shot a bird or caught a deer in his trap, boasting and bragging day in, day out. Every sentence ended with, 'It's me, me, me, Goat; it's me, Mr. Goat; it's me, the great hunter, Goat.'

One day Goat went off into the forest. He had not gone far when he saw a plump bird perched on a tree, spreading its wings, warming itself in the morning sun. Goat took aim, fired, and shot the bird. It fell through the branches of a cedar-tree into a small divi-divi tree and hung there, as if it were waiting for Goat to take it. Goat was very pleased with himself, planning how to make it known in the village that with his first shot, even without taking careful aim, he had hit the bird from a great distance.

Goat pulled the bird out of the small divi-divi tree. Its body was very light, no weight at all! But even while he hung the bird over his shoulder it began to change, the white and grey feathers falling away from the plump breast, the brown and grey feathers falling away from the wing, the loveliness changing into skin and bone. Dry-Bone! The weight on Goat's back grew heavier and heavier. Goat tried to get rid of Dry-Bone, racing beneath the low branches of a tree in order to knock him off, standing on his two hind legs, running fast then stopping suddenly with his head down, lying on his side on the ground, trying to shake off Dry-bone; but the skin-and-bone man clung to his back.

Terrified, Goat called for help. Snake heard him. So did Parrot, who flew off to find out what was happening. Goat's voice had never sounded like this. There was no boasting in it, no bragging, but desperate fear; for he could not shake off the skin-and-bone man.

'Who is calling?' asked Snake.

'Who is in trouble?' asked Dog.

'Mee, mee, mee,' cried Goat. He was too frightened and breathless to say more. Gone were the long sentences. 'Mee, mee, mee,' he cried. The animals rushed to his help and chased away Dry-Bone, but to this day Goat remembers. He boasts no longer. When he speaks, he says, 'Mee, mee, mee.'

Anansi knew these things. He should have been more careful when he met Rabbit and Guinea-Pig coming out of the woods. Rabbit had invited his cousin Guinea-Pig to go hunting with him. They had met at Rabbit's home under the shade of the gru-gru palm-tree. Packing a few hard biscuits and a bottle of water into a knapsack, they set off. Rabbit saw a bird sitting on a small divi-divi tree, spreading its wings in the warm morning sun, and he cried:

'Guinea-Pig, Guinea-Pig, I am in luck, in good luck, man!'

Guinea-Pig came racing through the high grass, shouting to Rabbit, 'Stop, it's Dry-Bone, it's Dry-Bone!' But while Guinea-Pig was calling to him, Rabbit shot the bird. It did not fall to the ground, but hung in the divi-divi tree as if waiting for Rabbit to pick it up.

'You have to carry it, Rabbit,' said Guinea-Pig. 'I promised to come hunting with you but I did not promise to carry anything that you shot. You have to carry Dry-Bone. I will carry anything else that we shoot.'

So Rabbit had to carry Dry-Bone. They put the bird into a bag, which Rabbit threw over his shoulder. Guinea-Pig helped to put the bag on Rabbit's back so that it hung comfortably, but he noticed that it was getting heavier. They set out for home, Guinea-Pig carrying the gun. Rabbit was very worried. He felt the increasing pressure of the bag on his back. There was no doubt that he was carrying Dry-Bone, and he did not know how to get rid of him. Worry wrote its lines over his face. As they went along the burden grew heavier.

'Help me with this skin-and-bone man,' said Rabbit.

'That is the one thing that I can't help you with,' replied Guinea-Pig. 'I will help you with any other burden, but not with this one. No Dry-Bone is going on my back.'

The burden on Rabbit's back was now so heavy that he walked with difficulty. He tried to throw away the bag, but Dry-Bone clung to him. From the bag came a thin voice, like the whisper of wind stirring dead bamboo leaves in the dry season when the ground is full of heat, saying:

'When you take me up, you take up trouble, you take up trouble, you take up trouble.'

Just then Mr. Anansi appeared in the distance. At the sight of him Guinea-Pig said:

'Cheer up, Cousin Rabbit. There is Anansi. You know what a greedy man he is! He knows that we have been hunting. Look cheerful, man, as if you have a lot of

good things in that bag. Look happy. I am sure he will
ask you for some of what you have.'

'He can have all that is in the bag,' said Rabbit.

'But don't start off by saying that, or he will suspect
a trick. Tell him we have a full bag, and that it is heavy.
Tell him we are both tired. Say that if he will carry the
bag a little way we will share what is in it with him.'

By this time Anansi was within shouting distance. He
knew that Rabbit and Guinea-Pig had gone hunting,
and he was hoping to get some of the birds they had
shot. He called out:

'Any luck, Yabbit?' (When he said 'Rabbit', he pronounced it 'Yabbit'.)

'Can't you see how heavy the bag is, Anansi?' asked
Guinea-Pig. (Rabbit was almost out of breath.) 'The
bag is heavy, man. I carried it part of the way and now
Rabbit is carrying it, but I wish we had help.'

'I would share what is in the bag with anyone that
helps us,' said Rabbit. He spoke slowly and with effort,
for the weight of the bag was almost more than he could
bear.

'Oh,' said Anansi eagerly, 'I'll give you a hand. You are my good friend, Cousin Yabbit. I know that if I help you, you will help me. Let me take the bag.'

Guinea-Pig helped Rabbit to put the bag on Anansi's back. 'Yes, this bag is heavy, heavy,' said Anansi, setting off down the road ahead of the others. Feeling the burden increasing in weight, he said, 'Brother Yabbit, what's in this bag that makes it so heavy?' There was no reply. Turning round, Anansi discovered that Rabbit and Guinea-Pig had disappeared. They had run away into the bush by the side of the road, glad to be rid of Dry-Bone. And a voice came from the bag, dry and thin like the whisper of wind in a field of dry corn when there has been a long spell of dry weather and parched red dust fills one's nostrils. Dry-Bone said:

'When you take me up, you take up trouble, you take up trouble.'

Anansi tried to throw the bag away. Dry-Bone clung to his back. Anansi hailed Donkey, who was passing, begging—

'Help me with this bag, Donkey, and I will share what's in it with you.' Donkey, who had been working all morning, replied:

'I am too tired, Anansi.'

So Anansi had to take Dry-Bone to his home. There Dry-Bone made himself comfortable. He said:

'Anansi, I will get off your back for a little while, but you must work for me, bring me food and drink, look after me, take good care of me. I have asked Mr. Rooster to keep an eye on you. I will pay him to do this. If you try to get away I will climb on your back again and you will never get rid of me. So, take good care of me, Anansi.'

This was trouble indeed! Anansi had not enough food in the house for himself, much less for Dry-Bone as well. He hated work. Now he had to work for the skin-and-bone man.

For a week Dry-Bone lived in Anansi's house. For a week Anansi had to work hard, feeding Dry-Bone and looking after him. On the eighth day, Anansi asked him:

'Dry-Bone, wouldn't you like to sit out in the sun?'

'Yes,' replied Dry-Bone in his thin, dry voice. So Anansi put the skin-and-bone man out in the sunshine.

Now Rabbit heard that Dry-Bone was with Anansi. Thinking that Anansi had suffered enough, he crept by, watching while Anansi lifted Dry-Bone out into the open air and warm sunlight. Anansi then returned to the house to cook the dinner. Rabbit crept close to the fence and called to him:

'Anansi, how are you getting on?'

'Oh, Yabbit, Yabbit,' pleaded Anansi. 'You must help me, man. You know we are friends. You can't leave me like this.'

'But what can I do?' asked Rabbit. 'I am not going to take Dry-Bone from you. What can I do?'

Anansi said:

'Run off to Fowl-Hawk. Tell him I have a man named Dry-Bone here in my yard. He must come to-morrow morning at this time, pick him up, and drop him in the thickest, farthest part of the forest. Fowl-Hawk is the only bird that doesn't fear Dry-Bone. I will pay him well.'

Rabbit went off, asking each animal he met where

Fowl-Hawk lived. He asked Rooster, but Rooster did not know; nor did Guinea-Pig. Indeed, Guinea-Pig told him that he should not worry about Anansi. 'Let Dry-Bone stay with him,' he said. 'He will teach Anansi how to work.'

Not until he met Guinea-Fowl did Rabbit learn the way to Fowl-Hawk's house. Towards evening he arrived at the place where Fowl-Hawk lived, and gave the bird Anansi's message.

The following day, at about ten o'clock in the morning, when the warmth of the sun was drying up the dew on the leaves of the trees, and the buds on the alamander and hibiscus were breaking into flower, Anansi said:

'Dry-Bone, shall I put you out into the warm sunshine?'

'Yes, Anansi,' replied Dry-Bone, 'and remember, when you take me up, you take up trouble . . . you take up trouble.'

'I know; I know,' replied Anansi; 'but you stay out here in the sun and warm your skin and bones.'

Anansi put Dry-Bone out in the sunlight, where the skin-and-bone man drowsed in the warmth, knowing that Anansi could not escape from him. Rooster was keeping watch on Anansi.

From far up in the sky Fowl-Hawk saw Dry-Bone sunning himself. Swooping down, he caught up Dry-Bone and carried him off before Rooster knew what was happening. When Rooster saw Dry-Bone disappearing he called out after him:

'Dry-Bone, Dry-Bone, where is the money you promised me for keeping watch on Anansi?'

But there was no answer. Anansi, looking up at the blue sky, now so clear and bright, sang:

> 'Carry him along, Anansi says so,
> Anansi begs so,
> Carry him along, Anansi says so,
> Anansi begs so,
> Carry him along, I'll pay Mr. Rooster,
> Anansi begs so,
> Anansi says so.'

How Crab Got a Hard Back

Now in the spring of time, when everything was new, there was an old witch-woman and nobody knew her name. She called herself Old Woman Crim, and though she was very rich she was very mean. She had no children of her own, but she kept animals as her children: Duck, Goat, Crab, and Peacock. These children knew her true name. Crab and Duck knew, and Peacock and Goat, but Old Woman Crim made them promise never to tell. Leaning on a long, crooked stick that she had cut from a tamarind-tree, and holding half a calabash full of magic water, she sprinkled the magic drops over them and said:

> 'Water, water, make bad things come,
> Who tells my name, I make him dumb,
> Water, water, make bad things come,
> I make him dumb
> I make him dumb.'

So Old Woman Crim's children never told her name.

The witch-woman had a voice that sounded like dry leaves when the wind blows them across the street. A thin, dry voice she had, and bright black eyes like beads, and a long, red purse in which she kept her gold. Old Woman Crim, as she counted her gold, morning and evening, said:

'I never spent money today,
I made them work right through the day
But I never spent money today.'

This was what Old Woman Crim did. She sent out
Parrot, and Kisander the cat, to spread the news that
she wanted a girl to work as maid and cook. The girl
had to work for a week. At the end of the week, if she
guessed Old Woman Crim's true name, she would get
half the clothes in the closet, and half the food in the
cupboard, and half the gold in the purse.

One girl after another came and worked. Each went
away without guessing the name. At the end of the rainy
season a girl from the town came and worked for a
week, washing the clothes down by the stream, cooking
the food, cleaning the floor, working from day to night
with Old Woman Crim saying in her dry, thin voice:

'Work harder, work harder through the day
Or I'll send you away, send you away.'

At the end of the week the girl went away crying
because she could not guess Old Woman Crim's name.
The old woman caught the tears in her magic calabash
and kept them there.

During the dry season another girl came and worked
all week, from sunrise till late at night, and at the end
of the week Old Woman Crim said:

'What's my name? What's my name?
Tell me the same.'

The girl guessed Quasheeba, Selina, Jestina, and all
the witch names, but she couldn't guess right. Old

Woman Crim sent the girl away hungry, and caught her tears in the magic calabash. So it went on till the witch-woman had the tears of a hundred girls in her calabash. And when it came near to Christmas no more girls came. There were no more girls to clean the house and cook the food and take Old Woman Crim's clothes down to the stream.

Try as hard as she could, the old woman could get no more girls. She sent out Parrot far and wide to tell the news. She sent out Kisander the cat to promise half the clothes in the closet, half the food in the cupboard, half the gold in the long, red purse. But no girl came.

Anansi heard Parrot calling the news from tree to tree. He heard Kisander the cat. Anansi wanted some money, for Christmas was coming. He said to himself, 'I can find out Old Woman Crim's name. I will dress up as a girl and work for her.'

So Anansi dressed himself up as a girl in a pretty white dress with pink spots, and a broad hat, and a little bag, and shoes with pointed toes, but not too pointed, for Anansi's feet were large—and high heels, but not too high, for Anansi couldn't walk easily in shoes with high heels. Then he set off for Old Woman Crim's home.

The witch-woman was glad when Anansi, dressed as a girl, walked up to the front door and asked for work. She had a lot of clothes ready to be washed. She took on Anansi, and said:

> '*The first thing to do, my daughter*—
> *Go wash these clothes in river water!*'

Anansi set off with the basket full of clothes and started to wash them in the stream. As he washed, he saw Crab walking along under the shelter of a rock. Anansi thought to himself, 'Ah, Crab is Old Woman Crim's child. He knows her name. I will find a way of making him talk.'

'Oh, what a pretty gentleman,' said Anansi, in a voice like a girl's.

'You like me, girl?' asked Crab. No girl had ever called him a pretty gentleman before. He was very pleased.

'You like me, girl?' he repeated.

'Yes, sir,' said Anansi, and smiled at Crab more with her eyes than with her lips, like a girl. 'Yes, sir. What a real dandy man, sir! Do you travel far?'

Crab was very happy, hearing how the girl in the white dress with pink spots praised him. He began to boast a little:

'Yes, girl,' he said. 'I travel all over the world. But you are a nice girl and you have a lot of sense, a lot more sense than any other girl I know. I like you, girl.'

'Oh, sir,' said Anansi, smiling more than ever, 'I like you too. If ever I get into trouble would you help me, sir?'

'Of course,' said Crab. 'If ever you get into trouble, girl, you come to me and I will help you.'

'Thank you, sir, from the bottom of my heart,' replied Anansi. 'But now I must go. I don't think you will see me again, but I will remember your promise, sir.'

'I never break my word,' boasted Crab. 'But I would like to see you again, girl.'

G   89

'Perhaps, sir, perhaps,' said Anansi as he walked away with the basket of clothes, walking very slowly because he was not quite used to the shoes with pointed toes and high heels.

At the end of the week Anansi was very tired. He had never worked so hard in all his life. Now it was Saturday and Old Mother Crim said to him, 'Girl, you have to guess my name. If you guess right you get money and food and clothes. If you guess wrong you get nothing.'

Anansi asked for a little time to consider. He went down to the river and sat by the rock where he had seen Crab. He took some of the river water and rubbed his eyes, so that it looked as if he had been crying. The drops trickled down his cheek like tears. He sobbed and whispered, 'Poor me girl, poor me girl! What am I to do.' He kept on sobbing and whispered, 'Poor me girl!'

Crab looked out from his home. He saw the girl in the white dress with pink spots, sobbing. He heard her whispering, 'Poor me girl.' He went up to her and said:

'Cheer up, girl, what's the matter with you?'

'Sir, I worked for an old lady the whole week and now she won't pay me if I can't guess her name.'

'Don't cry, girl,' said Crab. 'That's Old Woman Crim, my mother. I know her name.'

'Oh, poor me girl! Tell me her name, sir. Oh, what am I to do? Christmas coming and no money! Help me, sir.'

'Very well, girl,' said Crab. 'I promised to help you and I will.' Crab whispered the name in Anansi's ear.

Anansi never even waited to say thanks. He ran up the bank of the stream without stopping to pick up the high-heeled shoes when they fell off. He ran to Old Woman Crim's home so fast that he was out of breath when he got there. The witch-woman shrieked, 'Girl, can you guess my name?'

'I am not sure, ma'am,' replied Anansi.

'Guess,' screamed Old Woman Crim. 'Guess three times. Guess my name and you get the gold. Guess wrong and off you go.'

'Your name is Mother Jane,' cried Anansi.

'Wrong, wrong, first time wrong.'

Anansi said slowly, 'Your name is Mother Jonkanoo.'

'Wrong, wrong, second time wrong.'

'Guess again, then get along,' cried the old witch-woman, and now her voice was like the crackling of fire in dry bush. She held her purse tight, for she was sure she would not have to pay out any money. She shrieked:

'Guess again, then get along!'

'Your name is Mother Cantinny,' cried Anansi. 'Mother Cantinny, Mother Cantinny.' Anansi shouted the name aloud so that Parrot heard it and Kisander the cat also. Old Woman Crim fell to the ground as if she were dead. Then she got up, and gave Anansi half the clothes in the closet, half the food in the cupboard, half the gold in the long, red purse. As he went off through the gate, Anansi said, 'Anansi guessed your name, Old Woman Crim, old Mother Cantinny!'

Mother Cantinny was very angry. 'Anansi must have worked a trick on one of my children,' she said to herself. She called together Duck, Goat, Peacock, and Crab and stood them in a line. Then she said:

91

'They say that I am Cantinny,
They call me Old Crim,
I am Crim, you are Crim
And Cantinny,
Who said Cantinny?
Who said Cantinny?'

She looked into the face of each one as she asked, 'Who said Cantinny?'

She stared at Goat, and Goat stared back at her.

She stared at Duck, and Duck stared back at her.

She stared at Peacock, and Peacock stared back at her.

She stared at Crab, and Crab held his face down, looking at the ground.

'It's you, it's you,' she cried. She threw the magic calabash at him. Crab turned and ran, but the calabash fell on his back, and the tears of all the girls held it fast. There it is. That is how Crab got his hard back. Anansi made it happen.

Cat and Dog

Once, in the days when cat and dog were friends, Dog invited four cats to dinner. One of the cats was named Tatafelo, the second Finger Quashy, the third Jack-me-no-Touch, and the fourth Stumpy John because he had no tail.

Sad to say, Finger Quashy was a thief. She was a pretty cat, with a glossy ginger coat and yellow eyes. Her face, paws and tail were dark brown. The only touch of white was one long whisker on the right side of her mouth.

All cats move quietly, but Finger Quashy moved more softly and with more grace than Tatafelo, Jack-me-no-Touch, or Stumpy John, the slowest and most awkward of the four. So quietly did she move and so respectable did she seem, that no one suspected her of stealing.

The four cats were very pleased at being invited to dine with Dog. He was a good hunter and cooked well. Also, he had in his garden a large pear-tree with the

93

finest avocado pears in all the land. Dog's avocado pears fetched the highest prices in the market. The skins were rich purple, the seed small, the flesh of the pear a delicious, succulent butter-yellow. Avocado pear was the favourite food of the four cats so they licked their lips and curled their long whiskers when they thought of the dinner that they would have with Dog.

Finger Quashy was a little anxious about this dinner because she had been stealing Dog's pears. Not even Jack-me-no-Touch knew this, which was strange since Jack-me-no-Touch knew everyone's business. She was an honest cat, but a gossip, spreading tales and whispering stories, true or false. She began, 'Don't tell anyone, but . . .' and then she spread the latest rumour about Anansi, Snake, Rabbit, all the animals. She knew that someone was stealing Dog's pears for he had complained about this bitterly, but she never guessed that her own sister was the thief.

On the evening of the dinner the four cats turned up at Dog's home fully dressed. Finger Quashy and Jack-me-no-Touch wore long dresses and gloves, while the two brothers, Tatafelo and Stumpy John, were in tail-coats and top hats. Finger Quashy carried a very large handbag, much larger than her sister's.

Dog was very happy to see that the four cats had dressed for his dinner just as if they had been invited to the Governor's house or the King's palace.

Finger Quashy was relieved at the kindness with which Dog greeted her. She had feared that perhaps he had begun to suspect her of taking his pears. She had stolen twelve during the week, four on Monday, three large ripe ones on Thursday, and five others on Saturday.

Dog had been very angry, and had made it known that he would tear to pieces anyone whom he found in his garden. On greeting them he was so friendly, however, that Finger Quashy was sure he did not connect her in any way with the theft of the pears.

The four guests sat in the sitting-room with Dog, who complained bitterly that every time he picked a pear and put it down to ripen, someone stole it.

Finger Quashy said:

'Mr. Dog, you need a good watchman. I know that Rat loves pears. It may be that he is stealing from you. He is quick and clever. You will need a watchman to protect your pears. Only a very good watchman could possibly catch Rat. Why don't you employ me as a watchman?'

Dog thought this was an excellent suggestion. He replied, 'After dinner we will arrange this.'

After Dog left the sitting-room to get the dinner ready, Finger Quashy went to the pantry where she found two pears on a table by the cupboard, where Dog had put them in readiness for the meal.

Finger Quashy leapt on to the table and took up the two pears. She had not noticed that Rat was watching from under the cupboard. When Rat saw Finger Quashy stealing the pears he gave the alarm, shrieking:

'Dog, oh; Dog, oh; Finger Quashy is stealing your pears. Finger Quashy is stealing ... Finger Quashy is stealing your pears!'

But Finger Quashy was very quick. Dropping the pears behind a bush in the garden she leapt through the window into the sitting-room, taking her place in a rocking-chair before Dog could get to the room. When he entered he found Finger Quashy sitting quietly in the chair, looking very innocent and respectable.

Dog ran out of the room to the pantry. The pears were gone. Perhaps Finger Quashy had taken them, or Jack-me-no-Touch, or Stumpy John, or Tatafelo? No one else had come to the house. Certainly he would not give his dinner to the cats. Angrily he threw the food into the yard, picked up his walking-stick and ran back into the sitting-room; but the cats did not wait for him. They leapt into the yard and took refuge in a large tamarind-tree. There they sat while Dog raged beneath the tree, swearing at them.

'Oh, Dog,' said Tatafelo, 'I never touched your pears.'

'I didn't take your pears, Dog,' said Stumpy John.

'I am very surprised at the way you are treating us, Dog,' said Jack-me-no-Touch. 'You know that I am an honest cat.'

Finger Quashy said:

'Dog, what a bad man you are, swearing and shouting like this. I am ashamed of you.'

When Dog saw that he could not catch the cats, he started to walk back into the house. But his son had been playing with the fire in the open stove while he was out in the yard. Sparks from the fire had set the room ablaze. It was too late to save anything. Dog managed to rescue his little son, but he lost his house and everything except the one suit he was wearing.

Now Dog hates Cat—for it is on account of Cat that he has only one suit, the one he is born in and wears until he dies.

Anansi and Candlefly

THE bird Mancrow cast a shadow over the land and made darkness, but there were little ones in the forest and in the pasture near the village who took light with them wherever they went.

One was the little firefly Blinky, or Blinky Winky. He carried his light behind him, flashing it on every few seconds, but his light was feeble compared with that of Candlefly, who was much larger, and who cast a beam of light before her as she moved through the night.

By day or night Candlefly had fire. If Dog had to go out late at night he got Candlefly to go ahead and light the way through the bush. Whenever Mrs. Pig knew that she would be late getting back from the market she paid Candlefly to show her the way home. Briskly, not looking back, Mrs. Pig made her way safely past the deep hole by the mango-tree and through the fields of damp guinea-grass by the edge of the precipice that fell steeply, with jagged, sharp rocks, to the stream far below. Candlefly guided her home safely with her beam of light.

One day Anansi ran short of matches. He went across to Candlefly's house to ask for some fire, saying:

'Give me a piece of old firestick, Candlefly, any old piece that you don't want. It's time for my mother to start cooking the dinner, but we have no fire.'

Candlefly gave Anansi the fire and said:

'Anansi, I know that you are very fond of eggs. Would you like some?'

'You know that I love eggs, Candlefly; and when I went to Dr. Humming-bird the other day he said that I should eat as many eggs as I could get. That is what the doctor said, so I would be glad to get some eggs, Candlefly.'

Anansi went home with the eggs and fire.

On the following day Anansi went back to Candlefly. He said:

'I need more fire; and those eggs that you gave me yesterday were very good, very good indeed. When my mother tasted them she said they were much nicer than the eggs she gets in the market. Where do you buy your eggs, Candlefly?'

Candlefly gave Anansi fire, and four eggs, but did not tell him how she got the eggs.

Anansi was back the following day, asking for fire. Candlefly gave him the fire and one egg. He set off for home, but stopped half-way, put out the fire, ate the egg, and returned to Candlefly:

'Look,' he said, 'the fire wasn't good. It went out.'

Candlefly gave him fire. Anansi waited to see if she

would give him another egg. He waited and waited, but Candlefly went on with her work, paying no attention to him. Finally, he said:

'Cousin Candlefly, the fire is burning my hand. Give me one egg. If I put some of the egg-yolk on the burn it will get better quickly.'

Candlefly replied, 'Very well, Anansi, I will give you another egg, and since you like them so much I will take you to a place where you can get eggs easily, as many as you like. But you must not come until darkness begins to fall. I cannot take you to the place by day, only after nightfall.'

Next day Anansi walked about restlessly, waiting for evening. Before lunch he went to the village and borrowed from Shopkeeper Dog the largest bag he had. After lunch he kept going out of doors, looking at the sun, wishing that it would move more quickly across the sky. At three o'clock, while the sun was still high, he walked across to Candlefly's house and sat down to wait. Candlefly saw him sitting under a small ackee-tree opposite her gate and called out:

'That's a big bag, Anansi! But you will have to wait. We can't go to the place before nightfall.'

Anansi sat under the shade of the tree, picking away at the blades of guinea-grass and praying for night to come. He saw the sun sink slowly behind the mountain, and heard Cricket beginning to tune up in the bush by the side of the road. Anansi called out to him, 'You are a lazy fellow, Cricket, a lazy fellow. You should have started singing an hour ago!'

Tree-Frog began to whistle and sing from the branch of the ackee-tree, blowing himself up and then

99

whistling away. 'You, too,' said greedy Anansi. 'You are a lazy fellow, you should have started whistling an hour ago. Look how late it is!'

The first star came out in the indigo sky above, and the night breeze began to stir the leaves; a cool breeze that blows from the hills after sunset, laden with the perfume of logwood-trees, wild mint, and the heavy sweetness of night jasmine. To the star, Anansi said, 'Pshaw, you too lazy, too lazy, man! You should have begun to shine an hour ago!' To the night breeze he said, 'Shame on you! You have the whole day to sleep and you get up so late in the evening! A lazy good-for-nothing Breeze, that's what you are.' While Anansi had his mouth open, complaining and abusing him, Night Breeze blew a puff of dust into it, and went off down the valley laughing at the sound of Anansi sneezing and coughing.

'Ready now, Anansi,' called Candlefly, while Anansi was doubled up with sneezing. 'Ready. It's time to go!'

The two set off down the road, Candlefly going in front with her beam of light, Anansi following with his long bag. After walking for an hour Anansi and Candlefly came to Egg Valley. Every time Candlefly shone her beam on an egg, Anansi cried out:

'It is mine, it is mine; I saw it first,' and put the egg in his bag.

Soon Anansi had fifty eggs in his bag while Candlefly had none. Each time Candlefly found an egg, Anansi cried, 'It is mine, it is mine; I saw it first,' and Candlefly, being weaker than Anansi, could not take the egg away from him.

When Anansi had about a hundred eggs in the bag, Candlefly, who had none, turned to him and said:

'Mr. Anansi, since you are so greedy you will have to find your way home without a light. Good night.'

Candlefly flew home. There was no moon in the sky and rain-clouds covered the stars. Anansi was not sure which way to go, or where to put his foot. With his bag half full of eggs, he had to move carefully. He said:

'What a wicked creature that Candlefly is, going off with the light and leaving me in the darkness. Poor me, I must try to find my way home.'

Walking slowly, picking his way, straining his eyes to see what lay before him, Anansi set off and walked right into the side of a small house. The night was so dark that he did not see the building until he walked into it.

Not knowing whose house it was, Anansi called out, 'Godfather, Godfather, it's me, Anansi, come to see you.'

From inside came a voice that Anansi knew and feared: 'Who is that coming here at this time of night? Who is that?'

'It's me, Anansi, with some eggs for you, Godfather Tiger!'

'Wait there, Anansi,' replied Tiger. 'I will get a light. But if you are fooling me, if it is not true that you have brought some eggs for me, there will be trouble.'

The door opened. Out came Tiger, angry at having been awakened.

'Good morning, Tiger,' said Anansi. 'Here are the eggs I brought for you.'

'Good morning nothing,' shouted Tiger. 'It's not

morning, it's the middle of the night. Come in, and let me see the eggs. I don't trust you.'

Anansi entered the house and Tiger shut the door. The clock on the wall said half past one. Anansi put down the bag carefully, and showed Tiger that it was half full of eggs. 'Look at them, Godfather Tiger,' he said. 'Look what lovely eggs they are. I know how you like eggs. When I saw these I said to myself, "Godfather Tiger and Godmother Tiger will enjoy these eggs."

Tiger said to his wife, 'Put the large copper pot on the fire.' When the eggs were ready, Tiger said:

'Anansi, do you want any eggs?"

Anansi was so frightened that he said:

'Oh no, Godfather Tiger, I brought the eggs for you. I don't want any.'

Tiger and his wife began to eat the eggs, but knowing how greedy Anansi was, Tiger thought of a plan for finding out the truth. Sending Anansi out of the room into the kitchen for some water, he opened two of the eggs carefully, ate the contents, and put the two empty shells back into the pot, arranging them so that they looked as if they had not been touched. At the bottom of the pot he put a small live lobster. When all the eggs were eaten, Tiger said:

'Anansi, I am going to put out the light. You lie down here beside me.'

While Anansi was getting on to the couch beside Tiger, he saw the two eggs in the pot. He did not see the lobster. Then Tiger blew out the light.

Very quietly Anansi reached out, felt the rim of the pot, and put his hand down to take out an egg. The lobster bit him sharply. Anansi almost jumped out of

the bed with pain and
fright. Tiger asked:
'What's the matter
with you, Mr. Anansi?'
'Oh, nothing, nothing,
Godfather Tiger. It must
have been a flea from
your dog; something bit
me as I was falling
asleep.'
'Well, don't wake me
up again,' said Tiger.
Five minutes later Anansi

tried a second time to take the egg out of the pot.
The lobster nipped him more sharply than before,
and he cried out:
'My, my, what a lot of fleas there are in this bed,
what a lot of fleas!'
Anansi and Tiger passed a restless night. When
morning came Tiger said:
'You are the first man that ever came into my house
and complained of fleas biting him.'
Anansi replied:
'Godfather Tiger, I got very little sleep last night,
very little sleep. I feel tired now.'
Tiger's wife got breakfast ready, a light breakfast
since neither Tiger nor herself was hungry. They gave
Anansi a cup of coffee and a small slice of toast, then
Tiger said, 'I will go a part of the way with you. But,
Anansi, I am not so sure that I am going to let you go.
What were you trying to take out of the pot last night?'
Almost scared out of his wits, Anansi ran through the

door with Tiger after him. Seeing an empty gourd
Anansi dived head first into it and hid there. After a
few minutes Tiger gave up searching for Anansi, and
took up the empty gourd to get some water from the
stream.

'Brother Tiger, your mother is very sick, very sick,'
said a strange voice. It seemed to come from the empty
gourd.

Tiger looked around. He saw no one. He paused,
then set off again for the stream. Again a voice said:

'Brother Tiger, your mother is very sick. Come
quickly.'

Tiger heard the voice but saw nobody. 'I had better
run back to see if my mother is well,' he said to himself.
He threw down the empty gourd and hurried away to
his mother's home. Anansi crept out of the gourd and
ran home as fast as he could.

Anansi often tried to persuade Candlefly to take him
back to Egg Valley, promising that he would take only
his fair share, but Candlefly met each request with an
excuse; and Anansi is the only man to whom Candlefly
will not give a light.

Anansi's Old Riding-Horse

THERE was a time when Tiger walked on two legs. That was in the far-away days before Crab got a hard back and before Turkey got his bald head. In those days the Peacock had pretty legs to match his fine feathers, and Owl flew about by day and not by night. In that old time, Tiger walked on two legs, and all the animals bowed to him. Brother Goat bawled 'mee-eee-may-ay' every time he saw Tiger. That was how Goat said, 'Good morning, Mr. Tiger.' Monkey, who played tricks on everybody, never played tricks on Tiger because he walked on two legs and was strong. Every time Monkey saw Tiger he cried 'kee-kee-kee'. That was how Monkey said, 'Good morning, Mr. Tiger.'

Now in the village near Tiger's home there lived a pretty girl, Miss Selina. She could smile and she could laugh and sing, and when she smiled everyone loved her, Monkey, Goat, Sister Cow, and Mr. Anansi. When Miss Selina laughed, they loved her more than ever. When Miss Selina sang, then they loved her most of all. When Miss Selina sang, Goat, Monkey, and Cow sang just to keep company with her. They loved her so much that they sang loudly and out of tune, Monkey shrieking 'kee-kee-kee', and Goat bawling 'mee-mee-may', and Sister Cow calling out 'moo-moo-moo'.

But Mr. Anansi did not sing. He wanted to marry Miss Selina, and he knew that she would not like his voice if he started singing. No one in the forest liked the noise that Mr. Anansi made when he sang, so he listened while Cow, Monkey, and Goat joined in the singing with Miss Selina.

Tiger also wanted to marry Miss Selina. Every evening he walked down the road to call on her, dressed in his best suit, walking fast on his two legs. When he met Anansi at Miss Selina's he would say to himself, 'What a silly stupid this Anansi is, thinking that he has a chance of marrying Miss Selina when I am around.'

It was difficult to tell which of the two Miss Selina liked best. Now she would smile at Anansi and now she would talk with Tiger. Now she seemed to like Anansi best, now she seemed to like Tiger best.

One evening, before Tiger arrived, Anansi said to Miss Selina, 'Last night you talked a lot with Tiger, Miss Selina, as if you didn't know who he really is.'

'Why, Tiger is Tiger, of course! What else could he be?'

'Ah, but you don't know his history, Miss Selina,' said Anansi. 'I thought your friends would have told you.'

'History? I don't know what you mean, Anansi.'

'Didn't you know that Tiger was my father's old riding-horse?' asked Anansi.

Miss Selina didn't like the idea of getting married to anyone's old riding-horse. She was a proud girl, and very dainty in her ways. She said, 'Tiger is a fine strong man, Anansi. How could he be your father's old riding-horse?'

'Why, I used to ride him myself,' boasted Anansi. 'I used to ride him myself when I was small. Fine and strong indeed! I will prove that what I say is true.' Anansi hurried away while Miss Selina wondered what to do.

At that moment Tiger came in, dressed in his best suit, smiling and cheerful. Miss Selina said not a word to him. When he looked at her she looked away. When he spoke, she replied, 'Yes,' or 'No,' and looked away.

Next morning Miss Selina told Sister Cow, Goat, and Brother Monkey what Anansi had said. Goat went off and told Rat, and Cow went off and told Snake. 'Well,' said Snake, 'the only thing to do is to tell Tiger and hear what he has to say. But who will tell him? When Tiger is angry you know how he goes on, roaring and leaping all over the place.'

'Miss Selina herself must ask him,' said Rat.

When Tiger turned up that evening and found Miss Selina still unfriendly, he asked, 'Why, Miss Selina, what has happened?'

'Tiger, tell me the truth,' she replied. 'Are you Anansi's father's old riding-horse?'

'What did you say?' roared Tiger, forgetting for the moment that he was speaking to a lady, and springing up from his arm-chair.

'Not so loudly, not so loudly, Tiger. I only asked you a question.'

'That rascal Anansi, do you believe him?'

'But he says he can prove it, Tiger. I told Cow and Goat, and they told Rat and Snake. None of them can tell me if it is true. How can I marry anyone's old riding-horse?' cried Miss Selina with tears in her eyes.

Tiger rushed out of the house roaring, 'Bring Goat. Bring Cow. Bring Monkey. Bring Rat. Bring Snake. I will bring Anansi.' Even when he was out of sight Miss Selina could hear the roaring in the distance.

Anansi heard the roaring, too. He knew it was Tiger coming in a rage. He heard the noise drawing nearer and nearer. He could make out the words: 'Bring . . . bring . . . bring . . . Anansi.' The roaring grew louder and louder and louder, at first far off, then nearer, nearer, nearer: 'I will bring Anansi. I will bring Anansi. I WILL BRING ANANSI.' He scurried into his room, barred the door, barred the window, jumped into his bed, and wrapped his blanket round himself.

The heavy door shook as Tiger beat on it. 'Come out, Anansi,' he roared. Tiger rattled the door, shook it, threw himself against it. One hinge gave. Tiger kicked the door, beat against it, threw himself against it, and the door fell with a crash.

'I have you now,' he cried, while Anansi moaned and groaned in the bed, under the blanket. 'I have you now. I'll kill you for what you said. That's what I will do. To tell Miss Selina such a thing! I'll kill you! But first you are coming with me to tell them that what you said was not true. Up with you!' He caught Anansi by the foot and began to drag him out of the bed, Anansi groaning and moaning all the time, his eyes half-closed like a man who is near death.

'What did I say?' asked Anansi. He groaned, 'Ah, my back, ah, my stomach, oh, oh, my legs. I am going to die, Tiger. I ne-ne-never felt so bad in all my life.'

Anansi groaned and moaned in the most piteous way. A cold damp sweat came out on his forehead, and the whites of his eyes showed more and more.

Tiger left off roaring. Anansi did look like a man half-dead. He had to get him to Miss Selina before he died. Anansi had to tell her the truth, no matter how ill he was. He roared again, so loudly that Anansi shivered and moaned more piteously than ever, and said in a faint voice, 'Oh, my poor head; it's splitting with that roaring of yours, Tiger. I'll come anywhere, anywhere. I'll talk to anyone you like——' Here Anansi broke off, and shut his eyes and twitched his feet two or three times so that he looked nearer death than ever.

Tiger stopped roaring. He said, 'I will carry you if you can't walk, but you have to tell Miss Selina the truth. You have to tell her that I am not your father's old riding-horse.' Tiger began to roar again and Anansi began to shiver like a man with ague, and he opened and closed his mouth as if he were going to die. When Tiger saw how ill Anansi looked he stopped roaring, and said, 'I will carry you, and you will tell the truth and by that time, if you are not dead, I will kill you.'

'I will come, but you must carry—must carry. . . .' Anansi stopped. He seemed too weak to say more.

'You get on my back, Anansi. After you have told Miss Selina and Rat and Snake . . .' At this point, when Tiger thought how Anansi had said he was an old riding-horse, he opened his mouth to roar again, but when he saw how Anansi was shivering he broke off and said, 'Come! I will carry you, and afterwards, if you are not dead, I will kill you.'

'But, Tiger,' whispered Anansi, 'the blanket, the blanket.'

'What about the blanket?' shouted Tiger in a half-roar.

'Oh, oh, oh, my poor head, I am almost dead,' moaned Anansi. 'But I will do what you say. Oh, oh, the blanket, Tiger! Spread it on your back so I can sit on it. Oh, I am dying! I can never get there without my blanket to sit on.'

Tiger spread the blanket on his back and Anansi climbed up and sat on it, moaning and groaning. Tiger moved off, shouting, 'Stop that moaning! You tell the truth and, if you are not dead, I will kill you.'

'Tiger, Tiger,' groaned Anansi, almost falling. 'Tiger, let me fall! Let me die! Put me down. Let me die!'

'I won't let you die yet,' roared Tiger. 'You tell Miss Selina the truth and afterwards I will kill you!'

'Very well,' moaned Anansi. 'But if you don't want me to fall and kill myself give me that old piece of rope to hold on to.'

'Here,' said Tiger, thoroughly alarmed at Anansi's groaning and moaning. 'Here! I will tie this end round my neck and you hold the other.' Tiger hurried along, Anansi sitting on his back on the blanket and holding the end of the rope that was round Tiger's neck.

'Softly, softly,' groaned Anansi. 'Oh, oh, the wasps and flies. Oh, oh! I am dying, I am dying! Stop, stop, Tiger!'

Tiger could feel that something had gone wrong with

Anansi. His one thought was to get him to Miss Selina's house alive. 'What do you want, Anansi?'

'That little piece of stick—there, by the side of the track,' moaned Anansi, pointing to a thick stick. 'Just to keep away the flies . . . Oh, my back, my back! Oh, my stomach, oh, oh. . . .'

Tiger handed the stick to Anansi, and hurried along. He had to get to Miss Selina's house while Anansi was still alive.

At last! There was Miss Selina's house under the bamboo-trees. She was waiting there with Rat and Snake, Cow, Monkey and Goat. Now Anansi would have to tell the truth, thought Tiger, and then he would kill him.

Suddenly Anansi dug his heels into Tiger's sides. He tugged fiercely at the rope. He beat Brother Tiger with the thick stick. He shouted, 'Didn't I tell you, Miss Selina? Didn't I tell you that Tiger was my father's old riding-horse?' Anansi dug his heels harder than ever into Tiger's sides and shouted, 'Gee up! Gee up!'

Tiger was so ashamed that he ran as fast as he could past the house, towards the forest, trying to shake Anansi off his back. He got down on four legs because then he could run away much faster than on two legs, and ever since then Tiger has gone about on four legs. Ever since then Anansi has lived out of Tiger's reach, up in the trees. And as for proud Miss Selina, she married Mr. Peacock.

Why Women Won't Listen

ONCE upon a time, in the open savannah country beyond Anansi's village, there lived a couple with one daughter, a pretty girl; so pretty that every young man within forty miles came courting her. The girl refused to marry, saying that she was the only child in the family and that she preferred not to do so. She wished to look after her mother and father.

The father, impatient at the number of young men who were continually seeking him out to ask his daughter's hand in marriage, said to his wife, 'These people keep on pestering me. I am tired of them. We must do something to keep our daughter out of sight.'

The wife agreed and the couple built a large house in the woods, in a hidden place not easily seen. In this house it was arranged that the daughter should live, and that the mother would take her food to her: breakfast at ten o'clock every morning, dinner at four o'clock every afternoon.

When the house was ready, the father, mother, and the daughter, Leah, went to it after nightfall, choosing this time so that no one might see them. The parents lodged Leah in the house before daybreak. She wore a valuable ring of pearls and gold. 'Remember, Leah,' said her mother, when she was leaving the girl, 'say your prayers every night. When you hear this song you will know that I am coming with your breakfast, or your lunch. Open the door after hearing this song. Open it to no one else. Listen to the song:

> 'Leah, Leah, ting-a-ling-ting,
>   Honey at the door, darling,
> Sugar at the door, ting-a-ling-ting,
>   Darling.'

Now it happened that Tiger had watched the building of the house from behind a screen of bush and undergrowth. He was hiding under the house, listening to all that the mother told Leah.

At six o'clock in the morning the father and mother set out for their home.

The following morning, as soon as the mother reached the brow of the hill with Leah's breakfast, she sang her song. Leah pulled the double bolts, let her mother in, enjoyed the breakfast and gossiped till it was time for the mother to return.

Tiger had hidden under the house all the time, not stirring for fear of being heard. After the father and mother had gone he left his hiding-place very quietly, and made off at full speed for the Blacksmith's shop to ask him a favour.

'What favour do you want of me?' asked Brother Blacksmith, a very impatient man.

'Brother Blacksmith,' replied Tiger in his deep bass voice, 'there is a fat little fawn in the forest. I have been watching it for two days. I want you to file my voice so that I can speak sweetly, in a high note. Then I will be able to sing like the fawn's mother, and in this way I will be able to catch her.'

Brother Blacksmith said, 'This operation will hurt, Tiger.'

'I want a sweet voice,' replied Tiger. 'I will put up with the pain.'

Brother Blacksmith kept his iron in the fire till it was red-hot. Then he said:

'Tiger, open your mouth, open it wide.' Blacksmith thrust the red-hot poker down Tiger's throat. The iron hissed, and a cloud of steam rose from Tiger's throat.

'Now, Tiger, try a song,' said Brother Blacksmith. Tiger sang sweetly, so sweetly that he could not believe it was his own voice. He said:

'Thank you very much, Brother Blacksmith. I have to get used to my new voice.'

Brother Blacksmith said:

'Now, Tiger, eat neither orange nor guava. If you do, your voice will get rough and deep as it was before.'

Tiger hurried away, meaning to break into the house and eat Leah. As he went along he got hungry, for he had been hiding a long time under the house. Running through the woods on padded feet, he saw some guavas and oranges, and being very hungry, he said to himself, 'I am sure I can eat them. Blacksmith is stupid. How could guavas give me a rough voice?' Tiger ate, then tried out his voice. It was like thunder. 'Never mind,' he said. 'I will run quickly. The roughness will wear off by the time that I get to Leah.' He crept under the house till it was near to dinner-time, then ran to the brow of the hill and sang:

> '*Leah, Leah, ting-a-ling-ting,*
> *Honey at the door, darling,*
> *Sugar at the door, ting-a-ling-ting,*
> *Darling.*'

Laughing, Leah shouted through the window: 'That's not my mother. She doesn't have a bass voice.'
Tiger crept back under the house, his tail between his legs, ashamed of himself. Presently Leah's mother came to the brow of the hill and sang:

> '*Leah, Leah, ting-a-ling-ting,*
> *Honey at the door, darling,*
> *Sugar at the door, ting-a-ling-ting,*
> *Darling.*'

Leah opened the door, and let her mother in. Mother and daughter hugged and kissed each other, making much of their time together. Leah began to tell her mother what had happened when there came a great rolling, with a shaking of the ground. 'Hurry, Mother,' said Leah. 'Let's go home. I don't like to stay here by myself. Take me with you.'
'Your father wouldn't like me to do that,' replied her mother. 'But I will run home and tell him.'
The father said, 'Yes, of course she must come back if she is frightened. Hurry back for her.'

'I will go at the usual time tomorrow,' said the mother. 'She is quite safe.'

Next morning early, Tiger returned to Brother Blacksmith. 'Oh,' he said, 'I was very stupid. I did not do what you told me, but I was very hungry. Please push the hot iron down my throat again.'

Brother Blacksmith said, 'I have a good mind to hit you with the iron. Anyway, this time I can tell you the iron will be *very* hot. You will listen to me this time.'

Brother Blacksmith heated the iron for two hours, then pushed it down Tiger's throat. Smoke and steam poured out. Tiger leapt so high that he hit the roof of the Blacksmith's shop. Then Blacksmith said, 'Sing, so that I can hear if your voice is better.'

Tiger shut his eyes and sang. His voice sounded more sweetly than ever. 'Good,' said Tiger, 'I am off.'

'Remember,' said Brother Blacksmith, 'eat nothing on the way. If you do, your voice will become rougher than ever.'

Tiger said, 'Every time I see anything to eat I will shut my eyes.'

He hurried away to the house. Just before twelve o'clock he began to sing; his voice sounded sweetly, more sweetly than that of the mother. Leah opened the door. Tiger leapt inside and killed her. The ring of gold and pearls fell on the floor.

Leah's mother reached the top of the hill, and sang:

> *'Leah, Leah, ting-a-ling-ting,·*
> *Honey at the door, darling,*
> *Sugar at the door, ting-a-ling-ting,*
> *Darling.'*

No one answered. She sang the song twice. No one answered. She pushed the door open. Leah was not there, but she saw the ring on the floor. Full of anxiety, she ran back to her husband, who said, 'You will have to find the girl and give her to me.' At this the mother fell speechless, and died soon after. Taking to heart the loss of Leah and his wife, the father also died. That happened because women are so obstinate. Their ears are hard, so they do not listen, and because they do not do what they are told, this kind of thing occurs.

Anansi Hunts with Tiger

'Hush, hush, Anansi!'
'Why do you say "hush", Yabbit? I do not see . . .'
'Look! Look there!'

Rabbit was the first to see the wild hog. He was with Anansi in the cool woods at the foot of the hills, a long way from their home. At sunrise they had set out to find food. First they ran across the road, then across the field with the pond, and now they were near the hills.

Anansi looked, but he could not see the wild hog. Then there was a sound, far away; the sound of many feet.

'Into this hole, Anansi,' said Rabbit; 'hide here. If you make a sound, the wild hogs will hear us.'

Rabbit was full of fear. The wild hogs had long, bright teeth, and they liked rabbits. He hid in the old rabbit-hole at the foot of a tall tree, Anansi crouching beside him.

The noise grew louder, the noise of trampling feet, the sound of animals rushing through thick bush. Now they were very near. Five ran by, then six more, then a large band, so numerous that Anansi lost count. Two came so near that he saw the coarse black hair erect on their backs, their small wicked eyes, their gleaming tusks. Then the noise died away. Rabbit was about to leave the hole when another group of wild hogs rushed by, trampling the grass, crashing through the undergrowth. Alarmed, he remained in the hole with Anansi for a long time. When the sun was low in the sky, they ran out of the forest and returned home across the field.

That night, in his sleep, Anansi saw the wild hogs again, their burning eyes and curved tusks, and woke up with a cry. But when the morning came and the sun filled the house with light, he lost his fear.

'They give good meat,' he said to Rabbit.

'No, Anansi, I will not go with you to hunt the wild hogs. I cannot shoot and I do not hunt. Go to Dog or Tiger, and tell them of the wild hogs.'

When Dog heard of the wild hogs he went into the woods, but he did not take Anansi with him. He was away just over a day, and came back with a lot of meat.

That evening Anansi went to Dog's home, and heard all about the hunt. He could smell the meat that Mrs. Dog was cooking, but they did not share their meal with him. Anansi went home hungry. He longed for some of the meat, but since he could not get it by himself, he decided to seek Tiger's help.

Anansi came on Tiger in the shade of a tree, out of the heat of the sun. Tiger was half asleep.

'I am very glad to see you, Tiger; I have been looking

everywhere for you,' said Anansi. 'Have you heard about the wild hogs in the woods at the foot of the hill?'

'Yes,' said Tiger. 'I was here when Dog came back. That was a lot of meat he had.'

'Tiger, let's go out and get some of that meat.'

'Oh, I do not know that I want to,' said Tiger. 'I can get all I want to eat right here. You can go if you wish, Anansi. I will stay here.'

The next day Anansi went to Tiger again. He went the day after that, and he continued to visit Tiger, day after day, until Tiger saw that he would have no peace if he did not go with Anansi. He said:

'Very well, Anansi, I will go to hunt with you. We will set out at seven in the morning.'

Next day Anansi was up by six, with his old gun and his shabby knapsack. At seven he was at Tiger's house.

Tiger was up and about when Anansi came, and soon the two were on their way to the woods to hunt the wild hogs. The forest was a long way from Tiger's home. Anansi talked all the time, saying that he would shoot many wild hogs and that he was a little angry with himself because he had not taken a cart to carry all the meat.

'Did you know I was a good man with a gun, Tiger?' he asked.

'Not at all,' said Tiger. 'I was told that you could not shoot at all.'

This was true, but Anansi did not want Tiger to know that he could not shoot.

After some time they came to a place where the grass

had been trampled. In a field of sugar-cane near by most of the canes had been uprooted. Tiger said:

'Anansi, do not make a sound. We are near the wild hogs. Man-With-The-Gun may be there also and he must not hear us. If we make a noise and he sees us he will shoot. Do not make a sound!'

'As for Man-With-The-Gun,' said Anansi, 'I am not afraid of him. What can he do? I am not afraid of him.'

'You will not hear him, Anansi, but you will feel him,' Tiger said.

'I am not afraid of Man-With-The-Gun,' said Anansi. 'They say that he has a long whip, but I have one that can hit him as hard as his. If his can say "swish swish", my own can say "swishy swishy".' Anansi was about to show how hard he could hit with his whip when he heard a loud rushing noise.

'Here they come,' said Tiger. 'Have your gun ready.'

From where they were Anansi and Tiger could see the wild hogs. They were rooting beneath a young tree. Tiger made ready to shoot. Anansi went to a tree and rested his gun on a branch. When Tiger shot, Anansi shut his eyes and shot too. One wild hog was hit. All the others ran away.

'What a shot, what a lovely shot that was!' said Anansi. He went to the wild hog and cut it in two—the head for Tiger, the rest for himself.

A little after this they saw a wild hog eating by itself. Again Tiger took aim. Again Anansi went to a tree, rested his gun on a branch, shut his eyes, and shot at the same time as Tiger. The wild hog fell. Anansi

went to it, cut off the head for Tiger and kept the rest for himself.

'What is this, Anansi?' asked Tiger angrily. 'I do not think that you shot this hog. I do not think that you shot the one before this. As soon as I shoot a hog you run up as if you had shot it. Put your gun down or I will not let you come with me.'

'Well, Tiger,' said Anansi, 'no one can tell if my shot hit the hog or if yours did. I know that my shot hit this wild hog. Did you not see it fall when I shot? If I did not know that I killed it I would not cut it up.'

'Put your gun down, Anansi,' said Tiger. 'I think that you are trying to trick me. After this I will shoot and I will give you every other wild hog. In this way each of us will have half of those that I kill.'

Anansi said nothing. He was hard at work planning how to get all the wild hogs. He put his gun down, but as soon as Tiger shot he went again to the hog and cut off its head. Then he put the body in the bush and took the head to Tiger.

Tiger said nothing. He looked at Anansi, twitching his tail a little. Then he went on into the woods with his gun ready. All was still. The trees stood near together, as if to shut out the sunlight. Tiger and Anansi made no noise. They did not want the wild hog or Man-With-The-Gun to see them.

'Wait,' said Tiger, with his finger on his lips. Tiger pointed. Anansi saw a fat wild hog, fatter than any he had seen before.

Tiger shot the wild hog. It fell where it was and the noise of the shot went through the forest. Before Tiger could do anything, Anansi went to the hog and cut off its head. Tiger said:

'I said that I would not take you out of here, Anansi, if you tried to trick me again. You did not even shoot at the wild hog and now you go on as if it were your own. I am going. You will have to find your way out of the woods by yourself.'

Anansi was unhappy that Tiger should go on like this. He was afraid of being left in the forest by himself.

He wanted to leave, but not without the hogs that Tiger had shot.

Just then Anansi heard a noise.

'What's that?' he cried. 'Who is there? I have a gun and I can shoot.'

The sound came again, more loudly, and from another tree. Anansi was afraid. 'I have a gun here, I can shoot,' he said. But he could not see anything. It was hard for him to speak for he was afraid. He said:

'Co-come from near that tree so I c-can see you.'

There was no sound. All was still.

From another tree came the sound of a whip and of running feet. Then all was as before, very still. Anansi did not know what to do. He was afraid. The silence was broken by a noise from a fourth tree. He heard the noise of the whip and of the running feet; this time it was very near to him.

123

'Man-With-The-Gun,' said Anansi to himself. 'He will whip me.' He cried out:

'It's not me, Man-With-The-Gun, it's not me, it's Tiger that shot the wild hogs.'

The noise of the whip drew nearer. Anansi called out:

'Not me, not me, Man-With-The-Gun, it's Tiger. I have a gun but I cannot shoot.'

The noise of the whip came again.

'I cannot stay here any longer,' said Anansi. 'I must run, even if I have to go without the wild hogs. How I wish that Tiger were here!'

Anansi ran away. As he went by, each tree put out a branch to hold him back, but he ran on and on until he could run no longer. At last he was out of the forest. Now he could stop running, but he would not look behind him at all.

Far back in the woods, Tiger came from behind a tree with a whip in his hand. He was very happy as he went to the fat wild hog and put it into his bag.

'That's very good for Anansi,' he said to himself. 'I was right. Anansi never could shoot.'

With a smile on his face Tiger set off for home, his bag full of meat.

Work-Let-Me-See

Monkey's laughter mocked Anansi throughout the day. It followed him in the morning, on his way to Dog's shop to borrow half a loaf of bread. He walked quickly, hoping to escape from Monkey, but when he got to the shop, a burst of shrill laughter greeted him from a divi-divi tree:

'*Kee-kee-kee,*
Can't catch me !'

The stone that he threw fell short of Monkey, who leapt across to the tamarind-tree opposite, poked his small, wrinkled face through a fernlike screen of leaves, and started laughing again. Monkey's shrill 'kee-kee-kee' followed Anansi on his way to the stream where his mother was washing his clothes, spreading them on bare, hot rocks to bleach.

One Thursday morning, Anansi said to his wife and his mother:

125

'I am going away for a week, to stay with my friend Yabbit on the far side of the forest. Yabbit doesn't like Monkey, and I will get away from this singing-singing "kee-kee-kee" which is driving me mad.'

Taking a knapsack with him, Anansi set off, walking till he was tired, walking and sleeping until evening fell. That night he stayed with Rat. Next morning he set off early. What a relief it was not to be pursued by Monkey with his taunting song and mocking 'kee-kee-kee'.

But he was hungry. Eating one of the few biscuits left in his knapsack, Anansi fell asleep at the foot of a large silk-cotton tree whose silver-grey trunk rose like a great column built to hold up the sky.

On awakening, Anansi rubbed his eyes. In front of him there was an old iron pot.

'This is strange,' said Anansi. 'I am sure there was no iron pot here when I fell asleep. There are no footprints near by. How did it come here? I hope there is some food in it!'

But there was nothing in the pot! Anansi was disappointed. What was an empty pot doing there? He said:

'Iron pot, if you were any good you would have food. Somebody must have thrown you away because you were worthless. Why did they throw you away, anyhow?'

'Do not call me "iron pot",' a voice answered. 'That is not my name.'

Astonished, Anansi said:

'I didn't know that you could talk. I didn't know that you heard what I said. Who are you? What is your name? Why haven't you any food? Since you can talk give me an answer. What is your name if it is not "pot"?'

'My name is Work-let-me-see!'

'That's a queer name. First of all, you were not here when I fell asleep. How did you come here? Where did you come from? You are a pot, yet, when I call you a pot, you tell me that it is not your name. When I ask your name you give me the strangest name I ever heard. Well, prove that it is your name. I will call you by it. Go ahead, Work-let-me-see.'

At the words, smoke began to rise from the pot. Anansi watched in wonder, his appetite sharpened by the delicious smell of good food. What a meal he ate! Even his mother, who was a good cook, had never produced food so tasty, so satisfying. When he could eat no more he said, 'This is good. I need travel no farther. I will take this pot home. But first, I will wait until I am hungry and test it again, just to see if it really works.'

Later that afternoon, Anansi said, 'Work-let-me-see,' and again the pot cooked a meal. He told the pot, 'I am going to take you home. My mother will look after you. My wife and children will take care of you also. They will scrub you clean, for you look very dirty.'

'Do not wash me,' replied the pot. 'If you wash me I will not cook. Leave me as I am.'

'Then,' replied Anansi quickly, 'you may be sure that I will never wash you; and I will hide you from my wife, who loves to wash pots and pans.'

Anansi set out for home with the big iron pot. It was heavy and difficult to carry, but he had eaten well and carried his load happily, knowing that for the future, even during the hardest months of the dry season, he would not have to worry about food.

When Anansi got home he found that his mother, wife, and children were out. He hid the pot in a small room in the little house in which he lived. After settling the pot, he said, 'Work-let-me-see,' and shared out the meal, keeping it warm in the kitchen, ready for the rest of the family. How tired they looked, hot and hungry, when they returned from the village, and how excited they were at the sight of Anansi and the meal. 'Never cook for me again,' he told his mother and his wife. 'I will do all the cooking, but don't try to find out how I do it.'

On the following morning, Anansi went to the room where he had hidden the pot. Soon the smell of cooking filled the house. One of his sons looked through the keyhole, then ran off to tell his mother that he saw his father put his arm over a dirty pot and say, 'Work-let-me-see,' and that the pot started to cook breakfast.

After lunch Anansi went off to speak with his friend Dog, the shopkeeper. While he was away, his mother and his wife went into the little room, and his wife said to the pot, 'Work-let-me-see.' The pot cooked a delicious meal. After they had all eaten, she washed the pot, scrubbing it as clean as she could.

That evening, when it was nearing dinner-time, Anansi went into the room and said to the old pot, 'Work-let-me-see.'

Nothing happened. The pot did not start cooking. There was no smoke, no smell of food. No voice came from the pot. Then he noticed how clean it looked. His heart sank. Someone had washed the pot. 'I must hurry off to that tree,' he said, 'and tell the tree what a bad pot this is. I will let the tree know that the pot will not cook my dinner.'

Off went Anansi, travelling fast, so that he came to the silk-cotton tree early next morning. There was no sign of a pot. He sat and rested, slept, waked, looked around and saw a whip hanging from one of the branches of the tree, with a long lash and a handsome carved handle.

'What is that whip doing there?' he asked.

'Do not call me a whip,' replied a voice.

'How strange a thing this is,' said Anansi. 'First I find a pot that tells me it is not a pot, then a whip that says it is not a whip. What must I call you?'

'My name is Work-let-me-see.'

'Very well, then,' replied Anansi, 'Work-let-me-see.'

The whip hit him hard. He ran, and the whip ran after him. He hid behind the trunk of the tree and the whip found him; he jumped and the whip jumped; he climbed over the hedge that divided the field from the road and the whip climbed after him. He pulled the long, green leaf of the banana-tree round him, but the whip found him. He ran as fast as he could towards the forest, calling out for help, the whip chasing him.

There was only one thing to do. Anansi climbed a tree in the forest and took the shape of a spider. The whip climbed the tree but could not find him. It did not see the spider hiding under a green leaf.

The Sea-Mammy

A HARD time it was, a hard time after the hurricane had raged across the land, whipping the sugar-cane, blowing down the bananas, tearing branches from the trees, smashing through the forest to the sound of crashing trunks. The rain pounded down on the fields, scooping the young yams out of the brown earth. Hissing streams washed away the potatoes planted on the hill-side. Floods swept away the eddoes and coco plants in the valley. There was no food. The birds went hungry. Parrots shrieked for food, dogs tried to eat grass, leaves, and roots, and Anansi grew weak.

One day in those hard times Blackbird flew by Anansi's home. Looking at her, Anansi saw that Blackbird was fat. Her feathers were glossy, her hoarse voice sounded strong and clear, and she flew easily, like a bird that was getting its meals regularly. 'Blackbird has food,' muttered Anansi. 'I wonder how she gets it?'

Early next morning Anansi waited in front of his gate. As soon as he saw Blackbird he signalled to her to stop, and she said, 'I see you, Anansi. I am in a hurry but as we are friends I will stop for a minute, but not for long. I have not had my breakfast yet.'

'Breakfast,' replied Anansi. 'I have forgotten what breakfast looks like. As for lunch, the least said the better. As you will see, Blackbird, my clothes are falling off me.'

'Certainly you look very thin,' replied Blackbird. 'But why did you signal to me to stop?'

'Blackbird, do you get enough to eat? Where do you find food in these hard times?'

'I have a feeding-tree,' replied Blackbird. 'It is on an island out in the river, far from here. The only other person that knows that island is the Sea-Mammy.'

'Please, Blackbird, take me with you to the feeding-tree.'

'But, Brother Anansi, you have no feathers, so how would you get there? You cannot fly.'

'I am sure that I could fly if you would lend me some feathers, Blackbird. You see how thin I am. Once in the air, the breeze would carry me along.'

Blackbird picked out two feathers from her breast, two from the tail, two from the wings, two from the stomach. She stuck all the feathers on Anansi, saying, 'I will need these feathers, Anansi. When we get back please return them to me, for it took me a long time to grow them.'

'Indeed I will, Blackbird, indeed I will. But let's get moving: I am terribly hungry.' Anansi jumped into the air, and fell back to the ground.

131

'I don't think that you can fly,' exclaimed Blackbird. 'You had better let me have my feathers now.'

'Wait a moment,' said Anansi. 'All I need is a good start. Just before falling I felt the wind lifting me into the air.' He climbed on to the top of the garden gate, leapt off, and to Blackbird's surprise, circled round the garden once before settling back on the gate. 'See that, Blackbird,' called Anansi. 'I am hungry. Let's go.'

Blackbird and Anansi flew across the river to the feeding-tree. They ate as much as they could, and Anansi filled his bag with fruit from the tree. Early in the afternoon, Blackbird said, 'Time to go, Anansi!'

'Just a few minutes more,' begged Anansi. 'It's early. If I wait a little, I will be able to eat some more.'

Five minutes later Blackbird said, 'Time to go, I am not going to stay here any longer.'

'Oh, not yet,' pleaded Anansi. 'I am feeling hungry again.'

'If you won't come now,' said Blackbird, 'I will take away my feathers. I cannot stay any longer.'

'Take your feathers, then,' said Anansi. 'Leave me behind. I will follow.'

Having taken away her feathers from Anansi, Blackbird flew off in the direction of the setting sun, towards her home across the river.

Anansi kept on eating. Then he thought, 'I must go now, I am sure I can fly without feathers.' Jumping from a low branch into the air, he fell to the ground. 'Well,' he said, going down to the shore, 'if I can't fly I can swim. Let's see.'

Anansi jumped into the water with his bag of food. The cold, swift-flowing river carried him downstream

to the sea. There Anansi met
the Sea-Mammy who lived at
the bottom of the sea.

'Ah, Sea-Mammy,' said
Anansi, 'the river was too strong
for me. I was trying to swim
back to my home but it swept
me out to the sea. But I am not
sorry, for my mother has often
told me that you are my cousin.
Here, take this bag of food, and
since we are cousins, I want you
to help me to get home.'

'You will have to prove that
you are my cousin before I can
help you,' said the Sea-Mammy.
'I am going to boil a kettle of
hot water. If you can drink the
water you are my cousin. If you can't, I won't help you.
Come with me.'

The Sea-Mammy took Anansi through the water to
the island on which she lived. She put a kettle on
the fire and when the water was boiling she gave a
cupful to Anansi. 'Oh,' said Anansi, 'this isn't hot
enough. Put it out in the open, where the sun can make
it hotter, much hotter, then I will drink it.' The Sea-
Mammy did as Anansi said. She put the cup of boiling
water where the light of the sun could beat down on it.
There, as Anansi hoped, the sea breeze cooled it. Ten
minutes later Anansi drank the water, and said, 'There
you are. You see we are cousins, Sea-Mammy, so you
must help me.'

'That I will, Anansi, and thank you for the food you gave me. Here is your bag. Now I will call Tarpon to take you home.' Sea-Mammy called Tarpon, who brought his boat round, took Anansi aboard, and set off for the mainland. When they were about half-way on the journey, Sea-Mammy called, 'Tarpon, Tarpon, bring back Anansi, bring back Anansi,' for it had suddenly dawned on her that she had been tricked, and that Anansi was not her cousin.

'Ah,' said Tarpon, 'that's Sea-Mammy calling. She is calling me back.'

'Oh no, Tarpon,' cried Anansi, beginning to shout and sing. 'She says you must row quickly, a storm is coming. Row quickly, row quickly.' Anansi encouraged Tarpon and cheered him on while he rowed as fast as he could and soon reached land.

As soon as he set foot on dry land, Anansi said:

'Tarpon, I want you to weigh me. Hold this bag. I will get into it, and then you must lift it to see if I am light or heavy. I am afraid that I am losing too much weight.'

Born a Monkey, Live a Monkey

'*Kee, kee, kee,*
    Couldn't catch Monkey,
Kee, kee, kee,
    Couldn't catch Monkey,'

laughed the brown monkey from the branch of a
tamarind-tree that stood near Anansi's home.

Anansi was sitting in his garden, watching the green
mangoes on his tree, counting them and wishing that
they were ripe. Mr. Goat sat across the road talking to
his wife Selina, watching the shadows of the trees
lengthen as the sun set. Already Tree-Frog had begun
to say one or two words. He spoke and sang only when
brightness faded out of the sky and the first stars began
to shine. Monkey ran up and down the tree, laughing,
mocking Anansi:

'*Kee, kee, kee,*
    Kee, kee, kee,
Clever Anansi,
    Couldn't catch Monkey.'

135

He leapt from one branch to another, pointed a small
bony finger at Anansi, and sang:

'*Clever Anansi, clever Anansi,*
Couldn't catch Monkey, couldn't catch Monkey . . .'

Anansi rose and went into the house, slamming the
door angrily. Mr. Goat turned to his wife Selina, and
asked:

'Why is Monkey teasing Anansi like that? I thought
that they were good friends.'

'Yes,' replied Selina, stopping to nibble at a parched
blade of grass. It was the dry season. The earth was
dusty and brown, thirsty for water. 'They have been
good friends ever since Anansi saved him from Tiger
by telling Tiger how many brains he had.'

Mr. Goat laughed and said, 'But what has happened
to break up the friendship? You heard how Anansi
slammed his door just now. He must be in a terrible
temper. I am sure he is very angry with Monkey.'

'It happened this morning, while you were hunting
in the woods for food,' replied Selina. 'You know how
dry it is, and hot, with nothing in the market, and
everybody feeling hungry and praying all the time for
rain to come and for the grass to grow green again. It
was this morning it happened.'

'But what happened, Selina?' asked Goat. 'You tell
a story in such a strange way, saying it happened this
morning or it happened this evening, but not telling
me what happened.' Mr. Goat smiled. Selina his wife
always took her time over a story, just as she took her
time over the last juicy piece of lettuce leaf on her plate
when food was plentiful.

'Yes,' Selina went on, 'I was out in the garden and heard Anansi say to his mother, "Times are hard, and we have no food. The only thing left for me to do is to work. Oh, I hope things won't come to that. I only hope I won't have to work." '

Goat laughed. 'Never have I seen Anansi work, yet even when *we* are short of food Anansi seems to have some.'

'Well,' continued Selina, 'Anansi's mother comforted him, telling him that she was sure he wouldn't have to work because there were many people who wanted work and couldn't get it. She said he was safe.'

'Perfectly safe,' nodded Mr. Goat.

'Then Anansi told his mother that they would have to use their brains. After sitting out in the garden for an hour, thinking and thinking, they walked out of the gate down the road, Anansi in front, limping a little, resting his weight more on one foot, talking in his high voice all the time, saying, "Yabbit has no food and Cousin Snake can't help me," and so on.'

Brown Monkey dropped from the tree to the ground and sat beside Mr. and Mrs. Goat. 'I heard what you were saying, Goat,' he said, 'and I will tell you what that wicked Anansi tried to do.' He scratched himself with his hairy little paw.

'I was dozing in the bush by the side of the road this morning when I saw Anansi and his mother coming slowly down the track. I nearly called out to them, for Anansi was my friend ever since he saved me from Tiger, but I didn't, and it's a good thing I kept quiet.'

'A good thing indeed, or you wouldn't be here now,' said Selina.

'But what was a good thing?' asked Goat. He liked to listen to a story without any interruption. 'Go on, man. For the last five minutes I have been listening to you and Selina and I don't know yet what happened. I know only that you saw Anansi and his mother going down the track to the village.'

Monkey went on:

'When they came to the large mango-tree that stands by itself, Anansi told his mother to climb to the top of the tree. He climbed up after her, with a stick and a piece of rope. I heard him say to his mother:

' "I am going back down, but I am leaving the rope and stick with you. Every time you hear me sing a song you must do what I tell you in the song."

'I heard his mother say, "I will, my son, I will."

'I kept quiet because I saw that Anansi was up to some trick. . . .'

'He's always up to some trick, that Anansi,' nodded Selina.

'Shush, ssh, peace, wife, let Monkey tell the story,' said Goat.

'So I waited there, very quietly in the bush, and what do you think I saw? I can tell you that I was so shocked I nearly died from fright.'

'Go on, man, tell us what you saw, instead of telling us you nearly died from what you saw,' grumbled Goat. Selina patted her husband on the shoulder, and Monkey went on:

'Anansi left the stick and the rope with his mother, climbed down, and sat at the bottom of the tree. Sister Hen passed, looking for food in the grass, clucking every now and then. As soon as Anansi saw her he

called out, "Good morn-
ing, Sister Hen, how are
things?"

' "Bad, bad," said Hen.

' "Well, I can't com-
plain, Sister Hen. I am lucky. I live
up in the top of this tree with my
mother, and it's cool, cool. The breeze
is cool, cool indeed."

'Sister Hen asked Anansi, "But
what about food? I don't want cool
breeze, I want food!"

'Anansi told Sister Hen that he
had plenty of food at the top of the
tree.

'Sister Hen groaned with hunger
and said, "But give me some food,
Brother Anansi, give me some and I
will pay you back when the good
times come."

'What do you think Anansi did?'

'What?' asked Goat.

'Anansi, that wicked man, took
Sister Hen to the foot of the tree
and started to sing:

' "*Mama, I say drop the rope,*
Very well then,
Sister Hen stands here now,
Very well then,
Sister Hen stands here now,
Very well then."

139

'Anansi's mother let down the rope. Brother Anansi told Sister Hen to hold the end of the rope tight, then he sang:

> ' "*Mama, pull up the rope,*
> *Pull up the rope,*
> *Very well then.*"

'Anansi's mother pulled up the rope with Sister Hen holding tightly to it. When she was near the top, Anansi sang:

> ' "*Hit her with the stick I say,*
> *Hit her hard,*
> *Hit her with the stick I say,*
> *Very well then.*"

'That was the end of Sister Hen. Anansi burst out laughing and called out to his mother, "You see how easy life is when you have brains?"

'His Mother called out to him, "That is true, my son, and even though times are hard, Hen is fat, fat."

'Well, Anansi walked up the road whistling, and I saw that every animal he met was in danger. You know that little Rabbit goes down the road at the same time every morning. I was expecting to see Rabbit come running and jumping down the road, with Anansi waiting for him, so I ran round the bush and came walking along as if I knew nothing at all about Sister Hen.

'When Anansi saw me he stopped whistling and called out, "Good morning, Brother Monkey, my good friend." '

'Good friend, indeed,' said Selina angrily.

'SSush, ssush, Selina,' grumbled Goat.

'I told Anansi "Good morning", then he asked how I was, and how things were with my family. "Times are hard," I said, "very hard indeed, Anansi." He said he was lucky, like Sister Hen. I said, "But how are you so lucky, Anansi?" He told me that he was living at the top of the big mango-tree where it was cool, cool. Even at noonday the breeze up there was cool, and he could look out and see the whole world.

'Then he asked me about food. He asked if I had any, and, hearing that I had none, he said, "But I have food, lots of food."

'I said, "Please, Anansi, give me some."

'Anansi took me to the foot of the tree and sang:

> ' "*Mama, I say drop the rope,*
> *Very well then,*
> *Mama, I say drop the rope,*
> *Very well then,*
> *Brother Monkey stands here now,*
> *Very well then.*"

'The mother lowered the rope, and Anansi told me to hold it tight. He said his mother would pull me up, but I said:

' "Anansi, I can't go into a strange house first, that's not good manners."

' "But times are hard, man," said Anansi, "and you don't need to worry about manners. You go on first."

'I said, "No, Brother Anansi, my mother brought me up to have good manners at all times, good times and hard times. You go first."

'Well, we argued and argued till Anansi saw that I would not budge. Saying he would go up first and then let down the rope for me, he sang:

' "*Mama, I say pull up the rope,*
Very well then,
Mama, I say pull up the rope,
Very well then,
Your son Anansi stands here now,
Very well then."

'The mother pulled up the rope. When Anansi got to the top of the tree he called to me, telling me that I should follow him, and he sang:

' "*Mama, I say let down the rope,*
Very well then."

'When the rope touched the ground, Anansi said, "Your turn now, Monkey. Hold on tight." He sang to his mother, telling her to pull up the rope, but I wouldn't take hold of it. Anansi got angry. He called out, "Look, Monkey, I don't have time to waste, man, I have to meet Brother Yabbit in a little while. Come, hold the rope, hold it tight!"

'When I heard Anansi saying that he had to meet Rabbit I knew what he meant, so I burst out laughing. "Kee, kee, kee," I laughed.

' "Kee, kee, kee," Anansi shouted. "What are you laughing at, you stupid Monkey?"

'I shouted back, "It's you who are stupid, Anansi. Do you think I am Sister Hen?" I ran up and down the branches of the mango-tree, saying, "I don't need a rope to climb a tree, Anansi, and I don't mean to go the way of Sister Hen."

'That is why I am laughing at Anansi now.'

Remembering what had happened, Monkey began to laugh again and to sing out, mocking Anansi:

> '*Pull up the rope,*
>   *Clever Anansi,*
> *Pull up the rope,*
>   *Couldn't catch Monkey.*'

The door of Anansi's house opened and he shouted angrily:

'All right, Monkey, laugh away, laugh away. But you shall mock and follow fashion all the days of your life, all the days of your life you shall follow fashion. You were born a monkey, you will die a monkey, a follow-fashion monkey.'

From that day to this Monkey runs up and down the trees laughing at Anansi. If you ever hear him laughing, you will know why.

Mr. Wheeler

THE STORY OF HOW ANANSI ACQUIRED HIS LIMP

O NE day Puss set out on a journey. She loved
to travel, often spending days away from home,
exploring in the woods and through the savannah country. During her travels she lived by hunting, for she was expert in finding her food, her
sharp eyes marking quickly a lizard hiding on the
woman's-tongue tree, disguising himself by taking on
the white-grey of the tree-trunk or the dull brown of the
leaves that hung like tongues from the branches. In
all her travels Puss was careful not to cross a river or
set out to sea. She was afraid of water.

In the course of her journey, Puss came to a river.
She considered what to do. She wanted to get to the
other side, but could find no way of doing so. For two
days and a night she searched along the bank of the
river, looking in vain for a ford. Tired, she climbed a
tree that hung over the water and rested, looking at the
river.

Who should come by but Mr. Anansi, with fishing-rod and a bag for the fish. He fished for half an hour, caught nothing, sat under the tree, wiped his forehead, and said:

'This fishing is a bad business. I have to work too hard. Time to rest now.'

Looking around him, Anansi saw the dead stump of a tree. Something sticky was trickling out of a hole in the stump. Anansi touched and tasted the thick syrupy substance near the hole. It was honey.

'What a lucky man I am,' said Anansi; 'I have found a honey-hole.' Trying to get as much honey as possible, he thrust his hand into the hole. Something held him. He could not get his hand free. Frightened, he called out:

'Who holds me? Who holds me?'

From within the stump a voice came, saying.

'Mr. Wheeler.'

'Wheel let me see,' said Anansi.

The hand that was holding Anansi lifted him off the ground, wheeled him around seven times, and threw him fifty yards.

Fortunately for Anansi, he dropped on a large heap of dead leaves and tree moss. The fall stunned him so that he lay unconscious for a five-minute interval. If it had not been for the bed of leaves he would have been killed. When he came to himself he rose, shook himself, felt his hands and feet to see that no bones were broken, stretched himself, then said:

'Out of that little accident I see how to make a living for myself and my family.'

Anansi moved away the leaves and moss. He put in

145

their place a heap of stones and broken, sharp-pointed sticks. Then he went back to the tree-stump. Puss quietly watched all that was happening.

Sitting down near the stump, Anansi waited. After a little while, half an hour at the most, Peafowl came in sight. Anansi called out:

'I am glad to see you, Sister Peafowl. A living is here for me and you.'

'What is it, Mr. Anansi?'

'Come and I will show you,' replied Anansi. Rising, he took Peafowl over to the dead stump, showing her the hole and the honey, letting her taste how sweet it was, then said, 'Take as much as you wish, Peafowl. Push your right hand inside and take a lot.'

Peafowl pushed her hand into the hole. She called out:

'Anansi, something is holding me. I can't get my hand free.'

'Pull your hand away,' said Anansi. 'I will help you.'

Anansi took hold of Peafowl and they both pulled.

'Anansi, I can't get my hand away,' cried Peafowl, now very frightened.

'Very well then,' replied Anansi. 'Ask "Who holds me?"'

Peafowl did so, and a voice answered, 'Mr. Wheeler.'

'Peafowl, tell him "Wheel let me see."'

The hand wheeled Peafowl around seven times, then threw her so that she fell on the pile of broken rocks and sharp sticks. Anansi ran along with his bag, put Peafowl's body into it, and returned to his place near the stump. Before he could settle himself down, Mr.

Rat came strolling by, dressed very smartly. He was on his way to see Miss Mouse.

Anansi called out to him:

'I like to see a man dressed up like you are, Mr. Yat. I am glad to see you.' (Instead of 'Rat' he said 'Yat'.)

'I just bought this suit,' replied Mr. Rat, 'but it cost me a lot.'

'Well, I can show you an easy way to get money,' said Anansi.

'I wish you would,' said Rat. 'If I had enough money to live on, I would marry Miss Mouse right away.'

Anansi took Rat over to the stump, showed him the honey, and said:

'Put your hand into the hole. You will find the sweetest, thickest honey there.'

Rat pushed his hand in. Mr. Wheeler held him.

'Anansi, Anansi!' cried Rat, who was a very nervous man. 'Help me, man, help. Something is holding me.'

'Ask who holds you.'

'Wh-wh-who is holding me?' stammered Rat, who was so terrified he could hardly utter the words.

The voice from within the stump said, 'Mr. Wheeler.'

'Oh, Mr. Yat,' said Anansi. 'This is easy. 'Tell him "Wheel let me see." '

Mr. Wheeler wheeled Rat round seven times and threw him. Anansi ran along, picked up Rat's body,

put it in the bag, and returned. While Anansi was gone, Puss climbed down from the tree.

After Anansi had returned to his place near the stump, Puss came walking by. Anansi was very glad to see her, for Puss was plump and likely to be very tasty. He called out:

'Good morning, Puss. I am very glad to see you.'

'And why are you so glad to see me, Anansi?' asked Puss.

'Walk over here, my good friend Puss, my dear sister, and I will show you why I am so glad to see you. Come and see how we can both make a living.'

Puss went over to the dead stump with Anansi.

'Look at all that honey, Puss. Taste it.'

Puss pretended that she could not see the honey. She said, 'Honey, Mr. Anansi. I don't see any honey. Give me some to taste.'

Anansi touched the honey on the outside of the stump with his finger and gave it to Puss to taste. Puss said, 'Yes, this is very good honey, Anansi, very good honey. What a pity there isn't more of it. Now that you show me I can see it glistening on the tree-stump. What a pity there is so little of it. If there were a lot we could make a good living.'

'But there is a lot, Puss!' said Anansi angrily. 'There is a lot in the hole. Just put your hand in.'

'Anansi, I don't see a hole. Is it here?' Puss pushed her hand away from the stump.

'You must be blind, Puss,' shouted Anansi, who was fast losing his patience. 'My mother told me you were stupid, but I never believed her until now. Here is the hole, here.'

Puss pushed her hand in the other direction.

'Here, Puss, here. Watch my hand.' Losing his temper completely, and eager to catch Puss, Anansi accidentally thrust his hand into the hole.

Wheeler held Anansi's hand.

Anansi began to cry. Tears fell from his eyes. Thinking of the jagged stones and the sharp-pointed sticks, he cried out, 'Puss, something is holding me.'

Puss said, 'Ask who holds you.'

Anansi replied, 'I know who is holding me, Puss. Look, my friend, you know how I love you. I will give you everything in that bag if you will do what I ask you.'

'What is that?' asked Puss.

'Run along very quickly, Puss, along the bank of the river for fifty yards, to a place where there is a heap of rocks and sharp sticks. Move them away, dear Sister Puss, move them all away. Spread in their place as many soft leaves as you can find, just as if you were making a bed.'

'But, Anansi,' replied Puss, 'what a funny thing to ask. You are in trouble; you are my friend. I can't leave you alone.'

'I know what I am asking you to do,' said Anansi. 'And you must do it quickly. Pull some of the long, dead banana leaves from the trees and spread them out. Put some moss also. Make the place soft, soft.'

'Well,' said Puss, 'I really don't like leaving you here, but I will do what you ask.'

Puss ran along, and removed the rocks and sticks, though not all of them for she meant to teach Anansi a lesson. She spread the leaves and moss, but did not

149

quite cover the remaining stones. Then she hurried back. She found Anansi in a state of desperation, with beads of perspiration on his forehead. While she was yet a long way off, he called out: 'Did you do it?'

'Everything is ready, Anansi.'

'How do you mean that everything is ready?' asked

Anansi anxiously. 'Did you spread a lot of banana leaves, Puss?'

'Everything is ready, I think, Brother Anansi.'

'Look, Puss, you had better run back just to make sure. Run and bring me one of the banana leaves, so I will know you have done what I asked.'

Puss went away for ten minutes, and returned without the banana leaf. She said, 'Anansi, you must believe me. Everything is ready.'

Anansi felt the grip on his hand tightening. He knew he had no more time. Trembling, he asked, 'Who holds me?'

'Mr. Wheeler.'

'Whe—wheel—l-l-let me see.'

The hand wheeled Anansi round seven times and

threw him. He fell on to the bed of leaves, but he hurt his leg on the rocks that Puss had left beneath the leaves. Puss picked up the bag with Peafowl and Rat in it and went on her way home.

As for Anansi, to this day he walks with a limp.